BINGO

A novelization by A.L. Singer
Based on the motion picture written by Jim Strain

SCHOLASTIC INC.
New York Toronto London Auckland Sydney

TRI-STAR PICTURES PRESENTS "BINGO" CINDY WILLIAMS DAVID RASCHE
MUSIC BY JOHN MORRIS
WRITTEN BY JIM STRAIN PRODUCED BY THOMAS BAER DIRECTED BY MATTHEW ROBBINS
A TRI-STAR RELEASE
© 1991 TRI-STAR PICTURES, INC. ALL RIGHTS RESERVED

ISBN 0-590-45277-0

12 11 10 9 8 7 6 5 4 3 2 1   1 2 3 4 5 6/9

Printed in the U.S.A.   01

First Scholastic printing, August 1991

Chapter 1

There it was, just sitting there in a jar.

Its sweet smell floated out of the clown tent of the Hannibal-Hamlin Family Circus. Bingo stopped in the tent doorway. He dropped the bucket he was carrying and looked longingly inside. He could see it on the counter, all smooth and white and creamy and oh, so *cool*.

Clowns milled about, putting on their makeup and costumes. "Hungry, pal?" one of them said with a laugh.

The aroma was making Bingo dizzy with delight. He tried to stop himself from drooling. He tried to catch the hungry whine in his throat. But it was no use. He just couldn't help it — not when he was around his favorite food in the whole world.

Cold cream.

Now, cold cream isn't exactly the food of choice among most dogs. But Bingo wasn't like most dogs. For one thing, it was hard to tell exactly what he *was* — part collie, perhaps; part pug; part cocker spaniel. . . . He was a mutt, and his taste was as unique as his breeding.

Bingo's territory was strictly behind-the-scenes. No preening in frilly costumes for him, no standing on his hind legs on an elephant's back. No, Bingo was a work dog. Actually, *slave* dog might have been a better description. He got the water for the fancy dogs; he stood guard for them. During the shows he sat under the bleachers and watched *them* get all the glory.

Still, he wasn't unhappy. Before he joined the circus, he'd been homeless and orphaned. At least he had a job now, and he got to hang around nice people who fed him cold cream — like Billy the Clown.

Yip! Yip! Yip! Bingo barked at Billy and wagged his tail furiously.

"All right, all right," Billy said. "Don't they feed you in your tent?"

He tossed the cold-cream jar to Bingo. With a happy yelp, Bingo lapped it all down.

Behind Bingo, another clown poked his head in from outside. "Step on it, guys!" he called out. "It's rehearsal time — almost eleven o'clock."

Eleven o'clock?

Bingo suddenly lost his appetite. He had completely forgotten the chore he'd been sent to do. And he knew that if he didn't do it, he would be dog meat.

He scampered outside, picked up his bucket, and ran to a nearby water faucet. Placing the bucket under the nozzle, he turned the knob with his paw.

Water gushed out, filling the bucket. Bingo flicked the knob off and ran back across the circus grounds. He bounded off the Amazing Swami Rhamjani, who stayed fast asleep on a bed of sharp nails (proving once again why they called him Amazing).

Bingo scampered up to a trailer marked STEVE'S WORLD-FAMOUS HOLLYWOOD POODLES AND PENELOPE, THEIR PONY. Outside it, three white poodles turned to look at him through their sunglasses.

Yes, sunglasses. Marilyn, Lauren, and Betty were known as the world's most glamorous canines, and they looked it. Each lounged on a canvas chair lined with luxurious fur, shaded by a big beach umbrella, and cooled by a gently whirring electric fan.

Beside them stood Penelope the Pony, listening to a portable radio and pawing the ground to the beat of a song. One thing about Penelope — when she was into a song, she tuned out everything else. She didn't notice Bingo at all.

"Where's that mutt?" came Steve's voice from the other side of Penelope. "It's been thirty minutes! The water dishes are empty!"

Bingo took a couple of steps backward. Steve was scary. He owned the poodles and treated them as if they were his own children. Everyone else meant nothing to him — including Bingo.

"Give him a break," a female voice said. "He's been working all day."

Bingo wagged his tail. The voice belonged to Ginger, Steve's assistant. Bingo liked her. She was about a foot taller than Steve, brunette, and gorgeous — but, most of all, she was always kind to Bingo.

Bingo walked over to them. Steve was sitting on the ground, sewing sequins into Lauren's collar while Ginger cooked doggie burgers on a grill.

Putting down the bucket, Bingo barked.

The noise shocked Penelope. She whinnied and kicked wildly.

Splaasshhh! The bucket went flying. Water spilled to the ground, streaming across the tent . . . and right underneath Steve.

Steve bolted to his feet, a dark wet spot growing on his pants. He spun around, his face red with rage. "Why, you good-for-nothing, flea-ridden, worm-carrying mutt!" he snapped. "Look what you've done!"

Bingo shrank away. He hated when Steve got like this. He hated to do the wrong thing for Steve. After all, for all his faults, Steve was the one who had saved him from —

Steve grabbed an old, dirty sack and held it toward Bingo. "Remember this?" he said. "You want to go back in this? Back in the river where I found you?"

Going back. The thought of it brought a lump to Bingo's throat. When Steve had found Bingo in that sack, Bingo was practically starved to death. Steve gave him shelter, food, and a job. Sure, the shelter was a torn cardboard box under the trailer. Sure, Bingo ate only the scraps that the other dogs didn't want. Sure, his job was the most boring one on earth. Still, it was better than being dead.

At least that was what Bingo always told himself. But now, with Steve's blood-red face glaring down at him, Bingo wasn't so sure.

Just then Ginger's voice rang out from behind him. "Steve!" she cried out. "Something's wrong with Lauren!"

Bingo and Steve turned to see the poodle limping painfully toward them. Steve scooped her up in his arms and said, "Get Dr. Kendall!"

But Ginger was already gone. In moments she returned with the circus's veterinarian, who took Lauren and examined her paws.

With a quick yank, Dr. Kendall pulled out a bent, rusty nail. Lauren yelped in pain.

"No wonder!" Steve said. "Look at the size of that thing."

Dr. Kendall nodded. "Has Lauren been hanging around the Swami again?"

"Rhamjani?" Steve replied angrily. "Why, when I get hold of that guy, I'm going to hammer him to that stinking bed of his!"

"Slow down, Steve," the vet said. "Lauren will be just fine. I'll give her something for the infection, and she'll be ready to go in a couple of days."

"*A couple of days?*" Steve roared. "I've got TV executives coming tonight! They want to see a dog and pony show — and I have to give them the best. Without Lauren, we're dead!"

Ginger finally spoke up. "Why not use Bingo?"

Steve looked at her as if she were crazy. "Bingo?" he repeated. But before he even finished the word, his eyes changed. The fury disappeared. Maybe, he thought, just *maybe* it would work. . . .

And that was how Bingo became one of the Hollywood Poodles. That night, dressed in Lauren's costume, he made his circus debut. The crowd was small but noisy, and the TV executives were sitting front and center. Smells from the cotton candy and popcorn stands made Bingo tingle with hunger.

When it was time for the poodle act, Bingo strutted proudly into the ring. His costume was four sizes too tight, and he had never done any of the tricks, but he was actually excited.

Until the "Ring of Fire," that is.

When Ginger set an enormous hoop ablaze, Bingo went numb. When Betty and Marilyn jumped right through it, Bingo thought he would faint.

And when it was his turn to jump, Bingo froze. The ring and Ginger became one strangely shaped blur.

Steve, all dressed up in his ringmaster costume, cracked a whip. "What are you doing?" he cried out. "Jump!"

Bingo could barely hear him. He was flashing back to a time long, long ago — a part of his life he wanted to forget. In his mind, he saw the old, crowded pet shop where he had grown up. The shop was on fire, and Bingo was a puppy, shaking in a corner. Flames whipped up all around him as firefighters burst into the shop with huge water hoses.

They were just in time to save Bingo — but they weren't in time to save his mother.

The picture in his mind changed. Now he saw a small dog grave, freshly dug in a huge pet cemetery. On the tombstone it said TAFFY — BELOVED MOTHER. He saw himself standing next to it, howling with grief.

Steve's voice cut through the dream. "You're doing this on purpose!" he screamed. "You had it planned. You wanted to humiliate me. Come on, you little mutt — jump!"

But Bingo couldn't. Fire had taken his mother, and he wasn't going to let it take him — Steve or no Steve.

As the audience burst into laughter, Bingo just slinked away.

The act was over — but Steve's fury had only started. By the end of the circus, he was ready to burst. He stormed into the trailer with murder in his eyes, and Ginger had to sweep Bingo up into her arms.

"There it was," Steve ranted, his face twisted and tense. "Prime-time TV! My own series! All shot because that dog deliberately ruined my act!"

"You're wrong, Steve," Ginger pleaded. "He was afraid. Something about that fire scared him."

Steve stumbled out of the room. "Well, I've got the cure," he said.

Bingo could feel his heart start to race. Steve was rummaging around, trying to find something — but what?

When Steve came back in, Ginger let out a gasp. "Steve, you don't know what you're doing!" she cried.

But Steve wasn't listening. He lifted a large, brown hunting rifle — and pointed it right at Bingo!

Chapter 2

Ginger's eyes were wide with panic. "So he's not a circus dog, Steve. Is that a crime? He just needs a family that loves and cares for him. A little boy to play Frisbee with."

Steve looked through the gunsight, snarling. "*Frisbee?* The only thing this dog's going to catch is a bullet!"

"No!" Ginger shrieked. She quickly tossed Bingo toward the door, shouting, "Run for cover, Bingo!" Then, with a perfectly timed dive, she tackled Steve to the ground.

Bingo raced into the main room of the trailer. He grabbed a blanket in his teeth and pulled it into the back room.

Ginger and Steve were on the floor, swinging their arms wildly, each trying to get the gun. When Ginger saw Bingo, she said, "No, Bingo, not *covers*! Escape! Run for freedom! Do whatever makes you happiest!"

Bingo disappeared in the back room and came back with a tennis ball.

"Not *playful* happy — *fulfilling* happy!" Ginger shouted. "Go find a *family!*"

With a few powerful moves, Ginger grabbed the rifle and pinned Steve to the table with it — just in time to see Bingo come in with a photo of Ginger's family.

"No, you idiot!" she screamed. "Your *own* family!"

With a sudden growl of frustration, she yanked the rifle from Steve's hand. "You're right," she said to Steve. "Let's kill him."

Finally Bingo got the message. He sprinted out the trailer, with gunshots ringing out behind him.

His first stop was the clown tent. Billy was still there, late for rehearsal as usual. Bingo barked wildly, looking behind him every other second.

"You need to go, eh, pal?" Billy said with an understanding nod. "I figured this would happen someday." He pulled the tent flap closed. "Let me pack you some supplies — a little tent, some rope, cold cream, stuff you might need."

Bingo waited anxiously as Billy packed a duffel bag and a small backpack. Quickly Billy attached the pack to Bingo and put the duffel bag in Bingo's mouth. "Now, *go*," Billy said. "And don't look back!"

Bingo was loaded down, but he felt lighter than air. He ran and ran and ran and ran. Houses flew by, then long, flat stretches of land. All his fear was giving way to a great new feeling. A feeling of freedom and happiness that he had never had in his life.

Bingo had no idea where he was, and he didn't

care. Any place would have been fine — any place but the circus.

It happened that the circus was just outside of Denver, Colorado. It also happened that Denver was the home of Chuckie and Chickie Devlin, who hated each other and fought all the time — in other words, perfectly normal stepbrothers. They didn't know Bingo, and Bingo didn't know them, but that was about to change.

Soon none of their lives would ever be the same again.

A day after Bingo left the circus, Chickie powered his all-terrain bike across the woods behind his house, howling with excitement. His two best friends followed right behind on their bikes — skidding, wheelie-ing, spinning, hopping.

Behind them, pumping like crazy to keep up, was Chuckie. "Wait up, guys!" he called, almost out of breath.

Chuckie was twelve, two years younger than his stepbrother. He was also much smaller, and *much* less athletic. And Chickie never let him forget it.

Just ahead of the boys ran a narrow stream. Chickie raced toward it, speeding up. Along one section of the stream the bank was steep and slanted upward, a perfect takeoff ramp. Jerking his handlebars up, Chickie sailed off the ramp and landed clear on the other side of the stream. One by one, his friends followed him until they were all on the other side.

Then they all turned to look at Chuckie.

Chuckie pedaled furiously. His face was glistening with sweat — and his eyes were wide with terror. At the edge of the ramp, he pulled on his brakes. With a loud *sssshhhh*, the bike skidded to a stop, just short of the stream.

Chickie grinned at him. "What are you afraid of, you dork?" he said.

"Nothing!" Chuckie shot back.

"Then what are you waiting for?"

"Your body odor to evaporate!"

Chickie snorted a nasty laugh. "Let's go, guys. He's choked."

With Chickie in the lead, the boys tore off.

Their laughter echoed through the woods. It rang in Chuckie's ears. A burning sensation started in his stomach, slowly working its way to his head. He wasn't going to let them make him feel like a fool. He could do *anything* those jerks could do.

Gritting his teeth, Chuckie rolled backward, his eyes on the stream. Then, when he had enough starting room, he began to pedal.

His legs ached with the pressure. His wheel treads dug into the soft earth. The bike shot forward. It tilted upward as it hit the ramp. Chuckie stood up on his pedals and pulled up on his handlebars.

Had he pulled up a split-second sooner, he would have glided to the other side. Had he been a little heavier, or a little stronger, he could have built up enough momentum to make it.

But he didn't and he wasn't and he couldn't have been. His bike teetered in the air, then plunged downward.

Chuckie didn't even have time to scream before he came down headfirst on the sharp rocks below.

Chapter 3

Bingo loved the feeling of the soft forest floor. He sped along, his feet barely touching the thick bed of pine needles. When he got to the stream, he practically flew across.

And that was when he saw the sneaker.

It caught the corner of his eyes, a flash of white in the dark-green shade of the woods. It was attached to a limp, motionless body. Chuckie's body.

The moment his paws hit the ground, Bingo sprinted toward Chuckie. His heart pounded as he got closer. He could see that Chuckie was facedown in the water. There was no way to know how long he'd been there — but if it had been more than a couple of minutes, the boy was sure to be dead. Bingo dropped his duffel bag, clamped his jaw on Chuckie's pant leg, and pulled with all his strength.

Slowly the body slid out of the stream. Planting his feet on the soft earth, Bingo yanked and yanked until Chuckie was on dry ground.

But the body was still facedown, so Bingo dug his snout under it and pushed upward. Slowly, like a sack of potatoes, Chuckie rolled onto his back.

Bingo put his ear to Chuckie's mouth, but no breath came out. He touched Chuckie's neck but felt no pulse.

He didn't have time to think. If there were any hope at all for this boy, Bingo would have to act now. His mind raced back through his circus days, through the high-wire accidents and the collisions and the paramedics trying to save people. . . .

That was it! Bingo suddenly knew just what to do.

He scampered back across the stream and away from Chuckie. Then, dripping wet, he sprinted toward the takeoff ramp. He pounced off the ramp's edge, soaring over the water toward Chuckie.

With a dull thud, he landed full-force on the boy's chest.

The force was enough to knock the wind out of a conscious person. And it knocked a whole lot more than that out of Chuckie.

"Pkkkaccchhh!"

Chuckie sputtered. He coughed violently. Water gushed out of his mouth.

But he was alive!

Chuckie's eyes fluttered open. The woods were a blur to him, and there was a fuzzy thing in front of his face. For a moment, he thought he heard a dog bark. Then everything went completely blank.

When Chuckie awoke, he was naked and alone. He sat up and looked around. Slowly the woods came into focus. He was lying in a clearing, next to a small — *very* small — pup tent. A clothesline stretched from the tent to a nearby tree. Hanging out to dry were his clothes — and a dog collar.

On unsteady legs, Chuckie walked up to the collar and looked at the name tag on it.

"Bingo," he read aloud.

A loud bark pierced the silence. Chuckie spun around and saw Bingo for the first time, sitting at the edge of the clearing.

"Is this yours?" Chuckie said, holding out the collar.

Bingo barked again, and somehow Chuckie knew that meant yes.

"And you have a pup tent, too," Chuckie said with wonder. "Cool! Come on over here. I'm Chuckie."

Slowly Bingo walked over. He eyed Chuckie cautiously, wondering if he was a nice guy, or nasty like Steve. . . .

"That's it. . . ." Chuckie said in a friendly voice. "That-a-girl. . . ."

Bingo bared his teeth and snarled.

"Oh, sorry," Chuckie replied. "You're a boy, right?"

Bingo wagged his tail.

"You saved my life, didn't you, fella?"

Wagging his tail harder, Bingo began to whinny.

"All right!" Chuckie shouted. "High five!"

Bingo stood on his hind legs and raised his paw.

"You're amazing!" Chuckie said, picking up Bingo with a big hug. "I don't know where you came from, but you and I are going to be friends for life. Right?"

Bingo barked with excitement, then pounced on a stick and held it in his mouth.

"No time to play now, boy," Chuckie said. "I have to finish getting dressed and find something to eat. I'm starved!"

As Chuckie took his clothes off the line, Bingo darted into the woods. Before Chuckie could even get himself dressed, Bingo returned with a live trout in his mouth.

"Whoa!" Chuckie said. "You really are something!" He threw on his clothes and took the fish. Sitting next to Bingo, he felt his hunger slowly start to fade. But he knew his mom and dad sometimes ate raw fish at Japanese restaurants, and they seemed to like it, so . . .

After one bite, Chuckie knew he'd never trust his parents' taste again. *Bad-tasting* wasn't the word for it. *Nauseating* was closer.

"Go ahead, finish it," he said, tossing the fish to Bingo. "I — I had tuna for lunch."

Bingo eagerly bit into the trout and chomped away.

"Besides, from now on, *I'm* taking care of *you*," Chuckie added. "There're just two problems — Mom and Dad."

Bingo cocked his head quizzically.

"No pets allowed," Chuckie explained with a shrug. "But don't worry. I think I can handle it, if Chickie doesn't screw things up."

Bingo interrupted him with a loud bark.

"Chickie's my older brother," Chuckie said. "Sort of. He's my stepdad's real son before he got married to my mom, who's not my real mom because I'm adopted. We've got a complicated family."

Bingo suddenly stood stiffly, staring into the woods. There was a rustling of branches behind Chuckie.

"What's that?" Chuckie said, turning around.

"*RRRRRRRROOOOWWGHHH!*" A deep growl came from the bushes. Chuckie watched a hulking brown figure rise up, its teeth bared.

"A bear!" Chuckie cried out. "Sic him, Bingo!" But when Chuckie looked behind him, Bingo was gone. "Bingo! Where are you?"

"Rowf!" came a bark from above. Chuckie looked up to see Bingo in a tree. Bingo barked again urgently, as if he were giving Chuckie instructions.

For the second time, Chuckie felt that he could understand Bingo. The bear was after food — and there was only one source of food around. "The fish!" Chuckie said. "Right, Bingo!"

He snatched the trout off the ground and threw it toward the bear. As the bear knelt to pick it up, Chuckie quickly climbed the tree after Bingo. They both sat together on the branch, safely out of the bear's reach. Chuckie breathed a sigh of relief. He hoped the fish would satisfy the bear's hunger.

No such luck. An hour later, the bear was still there — and still hungry. Chuckie began singing an old song to pass the time: "There was a kid who had a dog and Bingo was his name-o. B-I-N-G — "

"Rowf!" Bingo barked in perfect rhythm.

"B-I-N-G — "

"Rowf!"

"B-I-N-G — "

"Rowf!"

"And Bingo was his name!"

Chuckie screamed with laughter and gave Bingo a high five. The two of them settled back and watched the rays of the setting sun filter through the branches of the surrounding trees.

Soon the ground was covered with shadows, and Chuckie couldn't be sure if the bear was still there. He picked a pinecone off the tree and threw it into the woods.

"Rrrrrrr . . ." came the bear's growl.

"No sweat, Bingo," Chuckie said. "Someone'll come looking for us. It won't be long."

But as the woods got darker and the sun set, panic began shooting through Chuckie. He cupped his hands to his mouth and yelled the first word that came to mind: *"Help!"*

His only answer was a heavy, sleepy silence. It took only moments for the night to swallow them up in pitch blackness. And Chuckie knew that even Bingo couldn't help him out of this one.

Chapter 4

The Devlins, minus Chuckie, sat glumly around the dinner table that night. The only noise was the chomping of the family jaws.

Chuckie's dad, Hal Devlin, wore a dark scowl — and not because Chuckie was gone. He was thinking about work.

Work, for Hal Devlin, was kicking field goals for the Denver Broncos. He was obsessed with his job. Even away from the stadium, he wore his jersey. He lived and breathed field goals, practicing them, thinking about them, talking about them. The Devlins ate off Bronco souvenir plates with Bronco souvenir silverware. Their house was decorated in the Bronco team colors. Hal Devlin had become famous for his barefooted kicking, and for years he had done it very, very well. But this season, something wasn't right. His foot didn't seem to have the knack anymore, and he had missed the goalposts eleven of his last twelve tries.

Whenever Hal Devlin missed, he became moody.

And when a six-foot, 180-pound father gets moody — the rest of the family *backs off*.

Natalie Devlin, Chuckie's mom, nervously picked up a fried-chicken leg and handed it to Chickie. "More chuckie?" she asked, then quickly added, "I mean, *chicken*, Chuck. I mean, chicken, chick . . . *chicken, Chickie!*" She sighed with relief. "There!"

Chickie turned away, making a sour face.

Mr. Devlin leaned forward. His bare right foot pressed down heavily into a Denver Broncos pillow on the floor. "Finish your chucken, Chickie," he ordered gruffly. "Chicken, Chuck — chicken, Chickie!" With a look of disgust, he turned to his wife. "*I* wanted pizza!"

Chickie smiled mischievously. "Chuck E. Cheese?"

Mr. Devlin threw his napkin on the table. "I don't need your attitude!" he barked. "I've had a tough day."

Mrs. Devlin had had enough of her husband's glumness. "Look, buster," she said, "don't start in with him. *He* didn't miss those field goals."

"First it's the coach, now you!" Mr. Devlin said. He lifted his bare foot up onto the table and began massaging it. "Why can't I get a little *sympathy* around here? The foot just doesn't feel right. It hasn't since the game with Buffalo."

"Leave your foot on the floor and the game at the stadium," Mrs. Devlin said. "Right now I'm worried about our son."

"Even if he is adopted," Chickie remarked.

Mr. and Mrs. Devlin both glared at him. "He's one of the family, who loves you very much!" they said together.

"Well, he's probably messing around in the woods," Chickie suggested.

"He could be lost!" Mrs. Devlin said.

"So why are you both getting on *my* case when *Chuckie*'s the one in trouble?"

"Will everybody cork it?" Mr. Devlin bellowed. "If we don't hear anything by morning — "

"Morning?" Mrs. Devlin said, her eyes wide with fear.

"Yes, morning," her husband replied. "If we don't hear by then, I'll call the police, okay?"

Neither Chickie nor his mother answered. They knew they couldn't reason with Mr. Devlin when he got like this. Still, they were both worried — even Chickie — and they knew that waiting till morning might be waiting too long.

"Good," Mr. Devlin said in the gloomy silence. Taking his foot off the table, he calmly added, "Now pass the chucken."

Hal Devlin may have been in a slump with his kicking, but he never let his principles sag. When he said "morning," he meant *morning*. Neither he nor Mrs. Devlin could sleep that night, but the newspaper said the Monday sunrise would be at 7:14, and Hal Devlin wasn't going to call the police a moment sooner.

"I don't care what the paper said," Mrs. Devlin said, looking out the bedroom window. "That's daylight out there, honest-to-God daylight. *I'm* calling the police."

"Hold it!" Mr. Devlin said, looking at his watch. "Just a few more seconds . . . fifty-six . . . fifty-seven . . . fifty-eight . . . fifty-nine . . . There! Seven-fourteen. I'll call."

He leapt off the bed and reached for the telephone. But just as he picked up the receiver, Mrs. Devlin called out, "Hal! It's Chuckie!"

Mr. Devlin dropped the phone and ran to the window. "I told you he'd be back!" he said, relief washing across his face. Then his expression instantly became angry. "I'm going to rip his arms off!"

"Hal, no!" Mrs. Devlin pleaded. "Remember what you said — no more negative attention!"

Nodding reluctantly, Mr. Devlin said, "How about one arm?"

Chuckie didn't spot his parents as he biked into his backyard. He had only one goal in mind: to get Bingo into the house without anyone noticing.

He hopped off his bike and turned around, expecting Bingo to be right behind him. But Bingo had his nose to the next-door neighbor's fence. On the other side was the neighbor's cocker spaniel, wagging her tail furiously.

"Hey, Dude," Chuckie said in a loud whisper, "this ain't the time to start flirting."

Bingo ran to Chuckie. Quietly they both sneaked through the Devlins' back door and into the kitchen. They tiptoed past the cupboards, heading for the hallway. If Chuckie could get Bingo upstairs into his room and hide him in the closet, then maybe . . .

Clomp! Slap! Clomp! Slap!

Chuckie instantly recognized his father's walk down the stairs — a slippered foot followed by a bare foot. Chuckie knelt down and shoved Bingo into one of the cupboards beneath the sink.

The moment the cupboard door closed, Mr. Devlin lumbered into the kitchen. "Morning, son," he said. "Sleep well?"

Chuckie couldn't believe his own luck. His dad didn't seem mad at all. In fact, Mr. Devlin simply walked out the front door, grabbed the morning paper, and plopped himself down at the kitchen table to read the sports section. Chuckie cringed when he saw the headline: DEVLIN SLUMP CONTINUES.

Soon his mom and Chickie came down. Mumbling "Good morning," Mrs. Devlin went straight for the stove, and before long the kitchen air was filled with the aroma of scrambled eggs and sausages.

Chuckie's feeling of relief disappeared. It seemed as if no one *cared* about what had happened to him! His mom put a heaping platter on the table, and he grimly spooned from it some eggs onto his plate. They looked perfect, but his appetite was gone. "Doesn't anybody want to know where I was?" he asked. "Do I need to have my picture on a milk carton first?"

"Finish breakfast, Chuckie," his dad said calmly. "I don't want you late for school."

"But shower first," Mrs. Devlin added. "You smell like a wet dog."

Chuckie thought fast. "That's because of the toxic-waste dump I fell into," he said, hoping *that* would get a rise out of them.

But no one seemed to be listening. He glanced quickly toward the cupboard where Bingo was hidden. Next to the cupboard on the floor was a small sausage link that had fallen from the platter.

Slowly the cupboard began to open. A mangy paw reached out toward the sausage.

Chuckie nearly choked on his eggs. Immediately his mom and dad looked at him with concern.

"Piece of shell," Chuckie mumbled.

Dinnng! A bell sounded directly above Bingo's hiding place. It was the toaster, popping up two slices. Chuckie's dad got up from the table to get them. Chuckie jumped from his seat. He ran to block his dad's path, stepping squarely on the bare foot.

"Watch the foot — that's your meal ticket!" Mr. Devlin snapped. "What are you doing?"

"Uh . . . toast!" Chuckie blurted. "I'm getting your toast!" He plucked the slices out of the toaster, making sure to block the cupboard from view. With a nervous smile, he gave the toast to his dad.

As Mr. Devlin walked back to the table, Chuckie's mind raced. He realized Bingo must have been starving — and dirty, if even Mrs. Devlin could smell the dog odor. Chuckie had to feed and wash Bingo. Now.

He looked from his stepdad to his mom to his stepbrother. Each of their heads was buried in a section of the newspaper. They wouldn't notice a thing — unless they looked up.

"For all you care," Chuckie said, trying not to sound nervous, "I could have been kidnapped last night."

"Pass the jam, Natalie," Mr. Devlin said without looking up.

Good. No one looked at him — they were *refusing* to look at him. Maybe this was some weird kind of punishment. Chuckie fought the urge to feel hurt; right now, Bingo was more important.

He snatched a few sausage links for Bingo. Then he opened the cupboard and pulled Bingo out. "What if I'd fallen into the hands of international terrorists?" he rambled on, pushing Bingo out the kitchen and toward the hallway. "Punk bikers? Ninja perverts?"

"More egg whites, Hal?" Mrs. Devlin asked nonchalantly.

Suddenly his dad's voice boomed out. "Hey! Just a minute, there!"

Chuckie froze. He imagined his dad drop-kicking poor Bingo through the living-room window. "I — I'm supposed to shower, aren't I?" he said, turning around.

"Aren't we forgetting something?" Mr. Devlin said. A huge grin spread across his face. He reached out with his beefy right hand and began rubbing Chuckie's hair. *"Chuckie, Chuckie, bring me luckie!"* he chanted.

Chuckie wanted to barf right there. He *hated* that.

"Okay, shower up," his dad said with a laugh.

As Chuckie ran upstairs, he smiled. Sure, his family didn't care whether he was dead or alive — but he had something better than family now.

He had Bingo, and he wasn't going to let him go.

Chapter 5

Pulsating and hot, the shower's stream felt wonderful on Chuckie's dirty skin. He felt like staying there the whole day. Just outside the shower, Bingo happily munched on the last of the sausage links.

A knock on the door made them both jump. "Chuckie!" came Mrs. Devlin's voice.

Bingo leapt into the shower. Chuckie yanked the curtain shut as his mom opened the door. "What?" he said, poking only his head through the curtain.

"Just getting dirty laundry," she replied. As she picked up clothes from the floor, she smiled at her son. Then, for the first time since Chuckie got home, she spoke with compassion in her voice. "About your father — he's having a very hard time right now."

"Tell me about it," Chuckie said. "One for twelve. Why can't he score?"

"I wish I knew," his mom said with a sigh. "Anyway, it's important that you know that he and I love you very much. Can you keep a secret?"

Chuckie nodded.

"We were really worried about you, honey," Mrs. Devlin said. "Of course, that's off the record and I'll deny it if you tell him, but it's true."

"Thanks, Mom," Chuckie replied.

Mrs. Devlin's brow scrunched up. She began sniffing the air.

Oh, great, Chuckie thought. She smells Bingo, and now she's going to pull open the shower curtain, find the dog, and humiliate him in the process. . . .

But all she did was walk out the door and say, "You wash extra good under those arms."

Chuckie practically collapsed with relief.

To everyone else in the Devlin family, it was a pretty typical Monday morning. Chickie rode his bike to the high school, Mr. Devlin got a ride to the stadium from a friend on the team, and Mrs. Devlin drove Chuckie to the junior high school.

Chuckie felt fine about leaving Bingo alone in the house. Bingo was a smart dog. What possible trouble could he get into?

Mrs. Devlin pulled the station wagon to a stop in front of the school, and Chuckie hopped out. He went to her window as she took a key ring from her shoulder bag. "Here's your latchkey," she said, handing it to him through the window. "Don't forget to turn on the oven when you get home after school. It'll take those potatoes an hour to bake."

Chuckie nodded, but he felt a sinking sensation. He knew why his mom wasn't going to be home when he got back. She was going to be at the local racetrack. He'd never been there himself, but he couldn't help but feel she was wasting her time. "I don't get it," he said. "What's so great about betting on horses?"

Mrs. Devlin had a sad, faraway look on her face. "Even a mom needs a little excitement . . . some sort of release," she said with a sigh.

Although his mom wasn't coming out and *saying* it, Chuckie immediately knew the answer to his question. His dad's mood swings had really begun to wear her down. If only his dad could start making those field goals again, then things would be back to normal, and she'd be happier. . . .

"Put it this way," Mrs. Devlin said, smiling, "if I win the Pick Six, it's Disney World this summer!" Then she gave him a twinkly, mischievous look. "Now, come on, don't you have something for me?"

Chuckie rolled his eyes in disbelief. "Aw, Mom, *here?* Give me a break!"

But Mrs. Devlin had that familiar rock-steady look in her eyes, and Chuckie knew he had to obey. Reluctantly he bent down so his head was near the window.

His mom reached out and tousled his hair. *"Lucky, Chuckie! Lucky, Chuckie! Bring good fortune to your Mummy!"*

As she let go and gave him a kiss, Chuckie decided to drop a subtle hint. "You know, Mom, some people think *animals* are lucky. I mean, not just for you and the horses, but for Chickie and his grades, Dad and his kicking . . ."

"Forget it," Mrs. Devlin shot back. "No pets!"

She waved good-bye and pulled away from the

curb. Chuckie exhaled with frustration. This wasn't going to be easy. Not by a long shot.

When school was out, Chuckie ran home as fast as he could. There was one good thing about his mom's gambling habit. It made it absolutely sure that Chuckie would come home to an empty house — empty except for the pet of his dreams!

"Bingo, I'm home!" Chuckie shrieked as he barged through the back door.

Bingo bounded down the stairs, yipping and jumping excitedly.

"Okay, okay!" Chuckie said with a huge smile. *"Let's jam!"*

He sprinted outside, with Bingo hard at his heels.

Their first stop was the video arcade in the shopping mall. Bingo leapt up and grabbed the joystick on one of the machines — and promptly trounced Chuckie at the game. They went from game to game, and Bingo won three out of four.

"Whoa!" Chuckie said. "What *else* can you do? Wait, I know!"

They raced back to his house. Chuckie ran inside and got his and Chickie's skateboards. As he maneuvered through the neighborhood streets, Bingo matched him move for move on Chickie's board.

Then Chuckie had a brilliant idea. He took the skateboards back inside and brought out his math books. "Now we'll *really* see how useful you are," he said to Bingo.

They walked to a nearby park and sprawled out

on the grass beneath a maple tree. Chuckie opened the book to his homework page and read aloud: "If a wheat field yields 46 bushels per acre, and the farmer is able to harvest 138 bushels before a rainstorm, how many acres of wheat has he cut?"

Bingo cocked his head for a moment, then pawed the ground three times. Chuckie scribbled for a few minutes, then looked up with amazement. "You're right!"

Chuckie let Bingo solve all his other math problems, which left them just enough time for a short fishing trip before dinner. They went home and Chuckie went up to his room and got his tape player with two sets of headphones. Then he grabbed some fishing gear out of the garage and loaded it onto his bike.

As he pedaled toward the nearby lake, Bingo padded along behind him. They set up at Chuckie's favorite spot, a grassy bank under a willow tree.

It was a perfect end to the afternoon — relaxing in the shade of the tree, listening to music, catching no fish.

When it was time to go, Chuckie stood up with a peaceful smile. He began loading up the fishing gear. "Bingo," he called out, "time to go."

Bingo was nowhere to be seen, but Chuckie wasn't concerned. Bingo had wandered away a couple of times to chase butterflies or explore, and that was probably what had happened again. "Bingo!" he called again.

No answer.

"Bingooooooo!"

Now his voice was echoing across the lake — and Chuckie was getting worried.

"Bingo, where are you? It's dinnertime!"

He shaded his eyes and looked all around. He listened carefully for the sound of footsteps crashing through the underbrush.

But he didn't hear a sound.

"Bingo!" Now Chuckie was panicked. Were there wolves in the woods? Coyotes? Could Bingo have wandered onto a road and gotten run over? His voice was choked with emotion as he yelled as loud as his could, *"Bingooooooooo!"*

Suddenly he heard a whimper behind him. He whirled around and saw Bingo climbing out of a trash can.

He had been hiding!

Chuckie burst into tears. He was so relieved — but he was also furious. "Don't you *ever* do that to me again!" he scolded.

Bingo hung his head in shame, and Chuckie's anger disappeared. As he looked into Bingo's eyes, he slowly began to realize why Bingo had pretended to disappear: He wanted to see how Chuckie would react. He wanted to find out how much Chuckie really loved him.

Chuckie thought about his family's reaction when he came home that morning. It had made him feel so small, so unwanted, so alone.

Chuckie realized that, in a way, he and Bingo were after the same thing — love. And even though Chuckie wasn't getting enough of it at home, he was determined to give it to Bingo.

He lifted Bingo from the trash can and gave him a huge bear hug. "I'm sorry, it's just . . . I never want to lose you. Okay? Promise me?"

Bingo happily licked his cheek. And it was in that moment that Chuckie knew the two of them were bound for life.

Chapter 6

Chuckie felt fantastic as he pushed his way through the back door of his house. In a loud, cheerful voice, he announced, "Hey, everybody, I'm ho — "

He swallowed back the last word. Standing rigidly in the kitchen were his mom, his dad, and Chickie. Their faces glared at him like stone statues.

Over their shoulders, Chuckie caught a glimpse of Bingo sneaking through the front door and up the stairs, exactly as he had planned.

"Something got into my cold cream," said his mom.

"Something chewed up my citizenship award," said Chickie.

"Something soiled our driveway," said his dad.

Chuckie felt cold sweat prickling out all over him. "What are you saying?" he asked. "That I'm hiding a . . . a dog?"

"Bingo," Mr. Devlin said.

What? How did he know?

Chuckie was stunned for a moment, until he realized his dad meant "Bingo" the way people usually said it — meaning "You bet!" or "That's right!"

"Sooner or later we're going to find him," Chickie warned, "and when we do — "

"That's enough, Chickie, *I'll* do the threatening around here," Mr. Devlin said. His eyes bore into Chuckie's. "You go to your room and pack your bags."

"Pack?" Chuckie said, flabbergasted. "Don't you think you're overreacting a little?"

"*Now*, young man!" his dad thundered.

Chuckie felt crushed. He knew they didn't think much of him, but *this* was —

Suddenly it dawned on Chuckie what had happened. He whirled around to his dad and said, "We've been traded again, haven't we?"

"We leave first thing in the morning," Mrs. Devlin said, bowing her head. "To Green Bay, Wisconsin."

"Green Bay — I knew it!" Chuckie said sullenly. "Just when we were getting settled. Talk about quick on the trigger!"

"That's enough!" his mom snapped. "Your father needs support, not criticism. Now go upstairs!"

Chuckie obeyed. As he walked into his room, Bingo raced happily toward him. "Easy, boy," Chuckie said. "I've got work to do."

He pulled a trunk out of his closet. It was the same trunk he'd used when his dad was traded from Dallas to New York, and from New York to Denver. Years ago it had seemed so huge, but now Chuckie's pants and shirts would barely fit into it.

"Chuckie, I brought you your dinner!" Mrs. Devlin called out, just outside his door.

Bingo dived under the bed as she walked in, carrying a tray of food. "Just pack enough to hold you for a few days," she said, looking at Chuckie's trunk. "The movers will take care of the rest."

"Can they take care of my insecurity?" Chuckie replied. "My lack of a stable environment? My sense of loss? My — my — "

"Dog?" Mrs. Devlin chimed in. Then she smiled and said, "Chuckie, I know you don't make friends easily, but pets aren't the answer."

"You adopted *me*," Chuckie said. "Why not a pet?"

"Because pets smell, and claw furniture, and carry disease, and make a mess in the driveway," Mrs. Devlin replied. "Maybe when you're older we can get a fish."

Chuckie sneered. "A fish? You can't *hug* a fish. You can't play ball with a fish. You can't fish with a fish!"

Mrs. Devlin shook her head and began stuffing clothing into Chuckie's trunk. "Boys your age think they have all the answers," she said. "Well, they don't — and they shouldn't lie to their parents!"

"Parents don't lie?" Chuckie said.

"Being a grown-up isn't easy, Chuckie. Not with house payments, urban crime, overdue bills, your father's run of bad luck . . ."

As her voice drifted away, Chuckie tried to cut his potato. But his knife could barely knick it. "Hey, what's wrong with this potato?" he asked.

Mrs. Devlin raised an eyebrow. "Somebody I know didn't turn the oven on when he got home. . . ."

"Oh . . ." Chuckie said, turning red.

"Anyway, the point is, son, we're a family, and we've got to stick together." Rearranging the pile of clothes, Mrs. Devlin pulled out a strange-looking leather belt. She held it up to look at the crude carvings hand-tooled on it: footballs, little shapes that looked like oak leaves, and the word *DAD*. "What's this?"

"It was supposed to be for Father's Day," Chuckie said, "but I screwed up the footballs, which is why I gave Dad the Old Spice."

"Why?" his mom asked gently. She held the belt with great care and admiration, as if it were covered with precious stones. "This is beautiful!"

"My crafts teacher thought I did a lousy job."

"*He's* not your father. And you know what? I think your dad could use some special cheering up right now." With a warm smile, she held the belt out to Chuckie.

Chuckie hesitated before he took it. "Are you sure?"

"Positive."

Taking a deep breath, Chuckie walked out of his room. He brought the belt to his parents' bedroom, where his dad was busy clipping his toenails.

"Hi, Dad," Chuckie said, holding the belt behind his back.

"Hand me that bunion cream, will you?" Mr. Devlin said, pointing toward a table full of tubes and jars. "It's the one on the end."

Chuckie picked up the jar and handed it to him. "Dad, I just wanted to say . . . look, I like being traded, okay? New kids, new hangouts, new . . . uh, *weather*. You know. Anyway, I want you to have this." He held out the belt. "It was supposed to be for Father's Day, but — "

Mr. Devlin took the belt and examined it. A flicker of a smile crossed his face. "You made this?" he asked.

Chuckie nodded.

"What are these round things — walnuts?"

"Footballs."

"Close enough." Mr. Devlin's stern expression seemed to melt, which made Chuckie feel warm and happy inside. "Nice work, son. I like it."

"Things will get better, Dad," Chuckie said. "You'll see. Sometimes when you need it the most, something special can come into your life and change your luck — something warm, something frisky, something so full of love that — "

"Thanks for the belt, son," Mr. Devlin interrupted, "but we're *not* getting a dog."

Chuckie was fed up. If his parents weren't going to let him have a pet, he would just have to hide Bingo for the rest of his life. As night began to settle, he furiously drilled holes into the side of his trunk. Air holes. Bingo watched him curiously, with his head cocked to one side.

"Don't worry, fella," he said to Bingo, "you're coming to Green Bay with me."

Bingo fit perfectly in the trunk. In fact, he decided to use it as a bed for the night.

Chuckie got ready for sleep, hugged Bingo goodnight, and got into bed. It was a warm, breezy night, and he left the window open. Who knew if the Green Bay air would smell as good as Denver's? He took a few deep breaths and plopped into bed. Then he dozed off peacefully, knowing that Bingo would be with him in his new home.

But as he drifted into a blissful dream, the top of the trunk slowly creaked open. Bingo peeked out until he was sure Chuckie was asleep.

Then, as quiet as only a dog can be, Bingo skittered out of the room and out of the house. He had some business he had to take care of. Important business with the cute cocker spaniel next door.

The next morning, Mr. Devlin hoisted Chuckie's trunk onto the top of the station wagon — and almost tossed it over. "Jeez, that's light," he said to Mrs. Devlin. "You sure that boy packed everything?"

Inside the house, Chuckie's urgent whisper echoed from room to room: "Bingo . . . Bingo . . . Bingo . . ."

He opened drawers and closets, cupboards and boxes. He looked in every pile of trash; he looked in the refrigerator, the bathtub, and the toilet.

But Bingo was gone.

Panic began racing through him. He began tearing the tops off boxes, pushing furniture over — until he glanced out the window and spotted the trash can in the backyard.

Of course! Bingo was playing his trick again! Chuckie ran outside and yanked the cover off the can.

No Bingo.

Chuckie felt as if his insides had been ripped out. In a few minutes, he was going to leave Denver forever — without the one thing in the world that mattered to him.

He was desperate now. He didn't care who heard him as he threw back his head and let out an anguished cry: *"Bingooooo!"*

But his only answer was the harsh, mocking *blat* of the horn on his parents' station wagon. Chuckie felt himself shrivel like an autumn leaf ready to fall from a tree.

It figured. Just as his life was beginning to have some meaning, it was all being snatched away from him. Even Bingo had betrayed him.

Defeated and depressed, Chuckie slumped toward the front of the house. He was too weak to cry.

Chapter 7

"Buck up, son," Mr. Devlin said, closing the station wagon's tailgate. "Wisconsin's got great . . . cheese."

Chuckie wiped the tears away from his face and nodded. He sat in the backseat of the station wagon, staring out the window, seeing nothing. Life had no meaning now. He would go to Wisconsin and count out the rest of his miserable days in cheese and bratwurst.

Mr. Devlin got in the driver's seat and started the car. As they pulled out of the driveway, Chuckie jerked forward.

And that was when he saw Bingo's face, peeking out of the neighbor's doghouse.

"*Bingo!*" Chuckie screamed, pressing his hands and face against the window.

Mr. Devlin glanced in the rearview mirror. "I should have known," he muttered. "It's a dog!" He floored the accelerator, and the station wagon tore out down the street. With a screech of tires, it turned right and sped into the distance.

"He'll never catch us now," Mr. Devlin said.

Chuckie's mom looked hurt and upset. "So there *was* a dog!" she said.

"I knew it!" Chickie piped up.

"Yes! Yes, there was a dog!" Chuckie yelled. He didn't care who knew now. *"Now stop the car!"*

"Speed up, Dad!" Chickie shouted.

Mr. Devlin sped through town like a running back through a field of blockers. He raced through intersections, wove through traffic, ran red lights.

Chuckie cowered in the backseat as cars swerved to avoid them. Before long, a chorus of car horns blared at them from every direction.

With each excruciating minute, Chuckie saw his last chance for happiness go up in smoke.

Mr. Devlin's mad dash had caused the biggest traffic tie-up in months — and Bingo arrived in town just in time to get stuck in it.

He scampered into the middle of the busiest intersection in town, sniffing the road for the station wagon's scent.

"Move that dog!" someone yelled.

"Is *that* what's causing all this?" screamed someone else.

"Run it over!" came another voice.

Bingo was so busy sniffing that he didn't hear the motorcycle cop screech to a stop behind him. But he sure did feel the iron grip of the man's hand on his shoulder.

"Chase cars at this intersection and you wind up with three legs," the cop said as he lifted Bingo into the air.

He carried Bingo to the side of the road, set him down, and looked into his eyes. "Well," he said with a smile, "you seem like a nice enough pooch, so I'm going to let you off with a warning. But if I catch you here again, I'll run over you myself!"

The cop got back on his motorcycle and sped away, and the traffic began moving again. With all the new motion and new exhaust, Bingo knew it would be almost impossible to pick up the Devlins' scent again.

But one thing was for sure. He would never stop trying.

The Devlins stopped two hours later at a roadside stand. Chuckie knew they were somewhere in the dead middle of the United States, but he wasn't sure exactly where. The stand looked like every other stand they'd seen along the road — old, decrepit, and surrounded by parked trucks and motorcycles. The only identifying sign said THIS IS IT! DUKE'S DOWN-HOME HOT DOGS!

Only moments earlier, Chuckie had been starving. But the minute they got out of the car, he lost his appetite. A horrible smell hit him like a solid wall. The outside counter was swarming with truckers and bikers, their boots grinding splotches of grease into the dirt. Behind the counter, dozens of grayish-brown weiners cooked on a grill.

The Devlins found four spots at the counter, and Mrs. Devlin picked up a frayed, stained menu. "You've got to be kidding," she said. "This is stadium food!"

"It's Americana!" Mr. Devlin protested. "These little places are getting scarce. You boys are going to try some roadside-trucker cuisine before it disappears forever!"

They gave their order to a bored-looking waitress with a name tag that said EMMA LOIS. She gave their order to a man with a beard stubble and a mouthful of chewing tobacco, who was standing near the hot-dog grill. "Here, Duke," she said. "For the tourists."

Duke picked four hot dogs with his hands and put them in plastic baskets lined with waxed paper left over from someone else's order.

Suddenly Chuckie felt sick. "I — I have to go to the bathroom," he said.

He quickly walked around back, hoping the wall would shield him from the stench. The stand was attached to a small, dilapidated barn. As he rounded the corner of the barn, he heard barking.

His heart began to race. Could it be . . . ?

The barking was coming from inside the barn — and there was definitely more than one dog in there. Chuckie walked slowly toward it, then opened the door and looked in.

His jaw dropped open. His stomach practically leapt through his mouth. It wasn't so much the smell, which was almost enough to knock him out.

It wasn't so much the sight of dozens of dogs pent up in wooden crates that were stacked along the wall.

It was the meat grinder.

It sat there like an old hulking monster, hazy in the dark mist of buzzing flies. Behind it, strings of sausage links hung like a curtain. When Chuckie thought about what must have been *in* those sausages, he felt himself starting to black out.

"Guaranteed fresh, partner," came a voice from behind the sausage curtain. A hand pulled the curtain aside, and Duke stepped through. "Or your money back."

Chuckie saw the sarcastic leer on Duke's face. He glanced at the blood-smeared apron around Duke's waist. He listened to the dogs barking helplessly in their crates.

And those were his last sensations before he hit the ground in a dead faint.

Chapter 8

"So it wasn't blessed by Ronald McDonald," Mr. Devlin said as they drove away from Duke's. "So what? No harm in eating a little dog meat. In some countries it's a delicacy. Nothing a little mustard can't fix."

Chuckie's stomach started to churn. He hoped his dad had finished talking about Duke's. He hoped no one ever mentioned the place again.

And judging from the looks on his mom's and Chickie's faces, he wasn't going to have to worry.

He sat back and let himself drift into a blissful dream about Bingo.

It was a good thing Chuckie couldn't see Bingo at that moment. If he could, the sight would have broken his heart. In the scorching rays of the midday sun, Bingo lurched along the side of the road, barely keeping himself up. Cars whizzed by him as if he didn't exist.

Not everyone was ignoring him, though. From above, a pack of vultures kept a careful eye on him, hovering hungrily, waiting for the moment he would stop moving.

Through sun-swollen eyes, Bingo squinted at a distant figure. It was walking toward him slowly, shimmering in the waves of heat that rose from the asphalt.

Bingo blinked once, twice. The figure's outline became clearer — the canteen hanging from his shoulder, the messy hair, the lopsided smile, the Denver Broncos hat.

Chuckie.

Bingo wagged his tail with his last ounce of strength. Chuckie broke into a sprint and lifted Bingo to his chest.

Whining with the parched remains of his voice, Bingo had only enough energy to paw at the canteen.

Chuckie set him down. "Thirsty, boy?" he asked. "Is that it?"

He unscrewed the canteen, then took off his cap and held it out like a bowl. Bingo felt weak with gratitude and he waited for his first sight of water.

But it wasn't water that came out of the canteen — it was sand! Bingo looked up with a start. A growl caught in his throat.

Chuckie had transformed. He was now Steve, cackling with sinister glee, holding out a torn burlap sack. "You want water?" he snarled. "I know a river . . ."

Suddenly the three poodles appeared behind Steve, looking on with satisfaction. Ginger was there, too, and she grabbed Steve's sack. "Steve, don't do it!" she shouted. Then she whirled to face Bingo with a twisted grin. "Let *me*!"

When Bingo woke up from his nightmare, he was lying on the roadside with a pistol in his mouth.

I'm still dreaming, he thought.

But he wasn't. His teeth clenched on the pistol barrel, cool and hard and definitely *real*. There was a hand clutched around it, with an index finger poised on the trigger. Bingo closed his eyes, too weak to do anything else. A mercy killing, he figured. Maybe it was the best thing that could happen to him.

The finger squeezed.

Bingo felt something shoot down his throat, something that seemed to take his skin with it. But he was still alive. In fact, he was beginning to feel better.

The finger squeezed again, and Bingo realized the gun was squirting liquid down his throat. It was a *water pistol*!

Bingo slurped and slurped. He felt life surging back into him. When the pistol was empty, a pair of strong arms lifted him into the passenger seat of an old pickup truck. Bingo snuggled contentedly as the truck started down the road.

A little while later, Bingo felt the truck stop. The man who saved him walked around to the passenger side and once again lifted Bingo into his arms. Through his half-conscious haze, Bingo could hear the barking of other dogs. At first his heart began to race with happiness, but there was something strange about the barking. Something urgent and not very happy.

"Another stray?" he heard a woman say. "Must be your lucky day, Duke."

Bingo craned his neck and saw the sign that read DUKE'S DOWN-HOME HOT DOGS!, and the haggard face of a waitress with the name tag EMMA LOIS. Then, for the first time, he heard the voice of the man who had saved him. "Get him some chow, darlin'," Duke said. "A few more pounds and he'll be perfect."

Bingo took a few steps around the back of the stand, and the barking got suddenly louder. He turned and saw the dog barn. Terriers, dachshunds, cocker spaniels, beagles — all were staring at him through stacked wooden crates with bloodshot, pathetic eyes. All of them looked as if they were waiting on some sort of Doggie Death Row.

It didn't take long for Bingo to figure out that they *were*. The sight of the meat grinder made him wish he had died in his sleep on the side of the road.

"Come along, little doggie," Duke said, pushing Bingo into a crate.

Emma Lois shook her head. "You're some rancher, Duke," she said dryly.

Bingo paced his crate, terrified. Duke had neglected to fill the plastic water bowl at the back of the crate, but Bingo had lost his thirst.

As the two humans left, Bingo listened to the frantic barking of a nearby terrier. It was a message, and Bingo understood it perfectly: *Look under your water bowl.*

Bingo walked to the bowl and pushed it aside. A gaping black hole was underneath. Whoever had been in the crate before him — may he or she rest in peace — had started it and gotten fairly deep.

Finish the tunnel, the terrier barked.

Bingo got to work. Strength seemed to pour into him. He dug with a frenzy, sending huge sprays of dirt between his legs.

The terrier kept watch, looking at the barn door with a small mirror he held in his paw.

Suddenly the terrier let out a squeal. He hid the mirror as the door opened.

Quickly Bingo slid the water bowl over the hole. He folded himself into a corner of the crate, trying to look weak and helpless.

Duke strolled into the barn, humming a song. In his right hand he held a meat cleaver, which glinted in the sunlight that filtered through the grimy barn windows.

Behind the meat grinder was a small, electric grinding wheel. Duke turned it on and pressed the cleaver blade to it. A sickening *shhhhink . . . shhhhink* echoed through the barn as red and yellow sparks flew.

Then silence, followed by the heavy tread of Duke's cowboy boots. Bingo held his breath. The footsteps were heading right toward him.

But Duke didn't stop at his crate. He went one farther — to the terrier. "Your turn," he muttered, leaning down to open the crate.

"*Aaaaaggggghhh!*"

For a moment, Bingo thought the sudden scream

belonged to the terrier. But it was too human, and too distant. And it saved the terrier from becoming a hot dog. Duke ran through the door that led to the kitchen, shouting, "What's the problem now, Emma Lois?"

Bingo heard Emma Lois ranting about cockroaches in the cupboard. Then he heard Duke arguing with her — and Bingo sprang into action.

He dug even more furiously than before. Soon his entire body disappeared into the tunnel. He felt the bottom edge of the crate's wall above his back, and he started digging up . . . up. . . .

Finally one of his thrusts broke through the surface. The sudden frenzied whining in the barn was deafening. Bingo began unlatching the crates, one by one. The dogs scampered out, yipping with happiness.

The crates were stacked high, and Bingo had to reach to get to the top layer. In the excitement, he began hurrying, swiping his paw carelessly.

With a huge *crasssh*, the entire wall of crates came tumbling down.

In the kitchen, Duke and Emma Lois froze. "What was that?" Duke asked.

Without another word, they pushed through the back door and into the barn. There, the dogs surrounded them. Barking and snarling, they forced Duke and Emma Lois into two of the large crates. Bingo himself latched them shut.

Working together, the dogs managed to push the crates outside and lift them onto Duke's pickup. The truck was facing the hot-dog stand, about thirty yards away. As the dogs began pushing the truck, Bingo jumped into the driver's seat and pushed down the clutch.

"You can't do this to me!" came Duke's hysterical scream from the bed of the pickup. "I'll get you for this!"

When the pickup built up some speed, Bingo popped the clutch. The engine started with a cough and a sputter, and Bingo hopped out.

He joined the other dogs, all of them happily watching. The truck barreled toward the stand. Duke and Emma Lois spewed curses.

Then came the crash. It resounded through the air like an exploding bomb. Glass flew, wood splintered, metal twisted.

And when it was all over, Duke's Down-home Hot Dogs lay under a ballooning cloud of dust.

Bingo looked at the other dogs. Each of them began barking, each with a different message. But each, in its own way, was doing the same thing.

Thanking its hero.

Chapter 9

Mrs. Devlin went into a three-point stance, nose to nose with Chuckie. Behind her, against the far wall of the motel room, was a thick net, rigged from the bed to the ceiling. Chuckie touched the football to the floor between his legs, ready to snap the ball to Chickie.

Hal Devlin went into his kicking stance, staring intently at Chickie's hands. When Chuckie snapped the ball to Chickie, he would kick the ball into the net — to an exact spot, if he was in good form.

"You figure it out, son," Chuckie's mom whispered to him. "We've averaged sixty miles an hour, times eight hours, times two days! How far away do you think that dog is?"

Chuckie let go of the ball. It rocked gently on the floor as he counted on his fingers. "Um, eight times five is forty, plus eight for six is forty-eight, times ten . . ."

Chickie began calling signals: *"Twelve . . . eighteen . . . thirty-two . . . seventy-six . . ."*

Losing count, Chuckie sighed with frustration.

"Okay, hundreds of miles," he said to his mom. "So what?"

"No dog could track you that distance," she said.

"*Hike!*" Chickie barked.

Chuckie was jolted back to reality. The football. He was supposed to snap the football to Chickie. They were in downtown Nowheresville. Practicing field goal kicking. In a motel room.

He grabbed the football and snapped it quickly. Too quickly. It sailed high, nicking the ceiling. Chickie leapt up, grabbed it, and pulled it down, just in time for it to meet the sharp kick of his dad's bare foot.

Thwapp! The ball sailed through the room, over Chuckie and his mom, over the bed, over the net. . . .

And out the motel window with a loud crash.

As the last of the broken glass tinkled to the floor, Chickie looked at his dad and shrugged. "Don't look at me. The snap was too high."

Somewhere along the highway, somewhere in the middle of the United States, Bingo wandered into a campsite. Barbecue smells made his stomach growl with intense hunger.

In the evening's waning sunlight, he wandered through the shadows of parked trucks, cars, and recreational vehicles. Between many of them were trash cans. Trash cans that seemed to beckon with the promise of half-eaten scraps of food.

He pulled down one of the trash cans, letting its contents spill out. As he rummaged through, a flashlight beam caught him on the side of the head.

Bingo cowered away. He glanced up to see the silhouettes of two men, one short and one tall.

"It's only a dog," the bigger one said.

"You're getting a little goosey, aren't you, Lennie?" the short one answered.

"Can you blame me?" Lennie snapped.

"Okay, okay. Club him and let's get some sleep."

"Club him? What's your problem, Eli? Didn't you have a dog when you were a kid?"

"Listen to you," Eli said. "What's next, Save the Whales?"

Ignoring him, Lennie turned to Bingo. "I bet you're hungry, huh, fella?"

Bingo barked enthusiastically.

"Smart, too!" Lennie said. "Come on, we'll get you some chow."

As they walked toward a nearby camper, Eli lit up a cigar. The match flame lit his face from below, casting eerie shadows on his scarred face. To Bingo, he looked like some horror-movie creature. He quickly hid behind Lennie's legs.

"Oh, don't mind Eli," Lennie said with a chuckle. "His bark's worse than his bite."

They stepped into the camper, and Bingo felt the fur rise on his back. Something was definitely wrong. Among the beer cans and junk-food wrappers scattered on the floor, there were also ammunition boxes, guns, and bundles of dynamite.

Who *were* these guys?

A glance to his left answered that question. Heavy sacks of money were piled against the wall, each stamped with the name of an armored-car company. Either they were employees of the company, or thieves. Bingo didn't have to guess too hard to decide which.

Eli picked up a dog-eared newspaper, folded open to the betting section of the sports page. He jotted some notes in the margin, scratched his head, and said, "Minnesota is looking hot."

"Oh, no," Lennie called from the kitchen. "You're not going to get us into a bet again!"

"Wait a second," Eli protested. "We can *double* our take if you let me put it on the Vikings against the spread."

"That's what you said last time," Lennie replied, "and we ended up having to pull another job to break even."

"Which is why this is perfect," Eli said. "It'll square us. Look at it this way: It's a *four*-point spread, on the very same night we find a dog with *four* legs. This is a lucky dog!"

"Do what you want with your cut," Lennie said, pulling a box of processed cheese out of the refrigerator, "but leave me out."

"Hey," Eli said, "I was going to use that for nachos."

"Nachos? You need *chips* for nachos!"

Eli frowned. He marched to a closet door and pulled it open.

Bingo stepped backward in shock. Inside the closet, bound and gagged, were a man, a woman, and two girls. Their eyes were wide with fright. "You got any chips?" Eli asked the woman.

She shook her head.

"That's okay," Lennie said reassuringly. "Don't worry, folks, we'll be gone after breakfast." He grabbed hold of the knob and pushed the door shut. "Forget the nachos. Let's turn in. Big day tomorrow."

Eli swept his arm along one of the camper's beds, sending beer cans clattering to the floor. Lennie did the same to another bed, then picked up a shirt off the bed and threw it to Bingo. "You curl up on this, fella," he said.

But Bingo was still staring at the closet door. It was a *family* inside there, an innocent family like the Devlins. *They* owned the camper, not Lennie and Eli. He couldn't just stand by while they were stuffed in there.

Click! Bingo spun around at the noise, and saw Eli pointing a gun at him. "Get away from there," he said. "Now go to sleep, or I'll put you to sleep."

Reluctantly Bingo curled up on the shirt next to Lennie's bed. Eli flicked off the light, and the camper grew silent.

Soon the stagnant air was filled with the rhythms of Lennie's and Eli's snoring. Bingo was wide awake. Directly above him, Lennie's fingertips hung over his body, barely touching his fur.

He carefully wiggled out from under the fingers. One step at a time he made his way through the obstacle course of trash, edging toward the only open window in the camper.

His foot brushed against a beer can. The tiny

clank sounded like a car crash in the nighttime quiet.

Eli rolled over, and Bingo felt the blood rush from his head. He sneaked a sidelong glance, hoping Eli would have trouble seeing him.

But Eli was still asleep, cradling his gun like a teddy bear.

Wasting no time, Bingo leapt out the window. He ran around the camper and bolted for the restroom complex in the center of the campsite.

There was a pay phone along the wall. It was Bingo's only link to the outside world. He pushed a trash can under the phone and climbed on top of it. Standing on his hind legs and reaching upward, he was able to knock the receiver off the hook. Then he used his right paw to tap out 911.

"Hello," came a tired voice. "What's the problem?"

"Rowf!" Bingo barked into the mouthpiece, which dangled in front of his face.

"Could you speak up, please?" the operator said.

"Rowf!" Bingo repeated.

"Okay, all I can hear is your dog," the operator said. "But my equipment has locked in your number and location. Are you in trouble?"

Bingo began pressing one of the buttons on the phone in a steady pattern: *Bip bip bip . . . beeeeep beeeeep beeeeep . . . bip bip bip. . . .*

He overheard the operator say to someone, "Dan, I think I've got a prankster calling from a pay phone on I-75. What do you make of it?"

"Hello? Hello?" came a male voice.

Bingo kept punching the pattern of beeps over and over. There was silence on the other end. Bingo hoped desperately they hadn't hung up on him.

Then, clear and loud, he heard the man's voice say, "Give me a pencil. It's Morse code!"

Eureka, Bingo said to himself. They figured it out.

He kept tapping out his message, the Morse code signal for SOS, until Dan shouted, "Got it! I'll call the police. Hang on for a few minutes if you can!"

A few minutes? What did that mean? How far away was the nearest police car? In this part of the country it could be *miles*. Bingo jumped off the trash can and noticed the campsite wasn't quite so dark anymore. The sun was beginning to peek over the horizon. He was sure Lennie and Eli would try to make an early break — and he didn't believe they would leave that nice family unharmed.

Bingo couldn't wait for the police. He had to try rescuing them himself.

He ran back to the camper and climbed through the window. Lennie and Eli were still snoring as he made his way to the closet. Standing on his hind legs again, he reached for the doorknob and turned it.

The door popped open. The family, curled and folded around each other in an uncomfortable sleep, started to stir. Bingo clamped his teeth on the heavy rope that bound them together. He pulled and gnawed, and slowly the rope came loose.

One of the sisters was the first to free herself,

followed by the other sister, the father, and the mother. They untied the bandannas around their mouths, then tiptoed across the room and out the door.

At the last moment, one of the sisters leaned back in to give Bingo a quick hug of thanks.

It was the wrong thing to do. The tip of her shoe caught the edge of a beer can, sending it clanking across the floor.

Bingo went rigid. So did the girl.

Behind them, Eli jumped out of bed. "Where do you think you're going?" he snarled.

His right arm clutched the gun, and pointed it straight at the girl's head!

Chapter 10

"EEEEEEAAAAAAGGGGHHHHH!"

The girl's scream was so loud, Bingo could feel his teeth chatter.

It was the perfect distraction. He leapt on Eli, swiping at his arm.

Crrackk! Eli fired his gun, but the bullet tore upward through the camper's roof.

In the confusion, the girl turned and ran through the door to freedom.

Bingo and Eli rolled off the bed, each struggling for the gun. "Lennie!" Eli screamed, desperately trying to throw Bingo off. *"Lennieeeee!"*

Finally Lennie rolled over. With a groggy yawn, he said, "I had the craziest dream. . . ."

"Lennie, get this crazy dog off me!" Eli shouted. He squeezed the trigger again, but the pistol was empty.

BANG!

A gunshot made both Eli and Bingo stop cold. They looked around to see Lennie with a smoking automatic pistol, pointing at the ceiling. "That's enough!" he said, angry and wide-awake. "I don't know which one of you started this, but you're both going to get us in big trouble."

As soon as he said that, a soft rhythmic *chucka-chucka-chucka* noise began outside. Lennie and Eli stared at the window, dumbfounded, as the noise quickly became loud.

"We know you're in there!" a voice blared over a loudspeaker. "Come out with your hands up, and nobody will get hurt!"

Eli ran to the window. His mouth dropped open at the sight of a helicopter hovering overhead, bathing the area with spotlights. Dozens of patrol cars were surrounding the camper, and cops were piling out, guns in hand. A television news van squealed to a stop just under the chopper, and camerapeople hopped out to set up.

"They've got us surrounded!" Eli said.

"We're okay," Lennie replied. "Why do you think we have hostages?" He ran to the closet and pulled it open.

Bingo laughed inwardly as Lennie gaped at the empty blackness. "What happened to them?" Lennie cried out. He looked at Eli, who was glaring at Bingo.

Slowly a look of hurt and betrayal spread across Lennie's face. "I took you in," he said to Bingo accusingly. "I *fed* you!"

Eli grabbed another gun, then snatched Bingo up in his arms and pointed the gun to his head. He went to the door and pushed it slightly open, enough so that the police could see Bingo and the gun. "One move," he shouted, "and the dog gets it!"

Bingo couldn't stop shaking. Surely the police would take Eli at his word. Surely they wouldn't sacrifice the life of an innocent dog who had single-handedly saved a family.

Wrong.

Gunfire blasted all around them. Bullets ricocheted off the camper. Eli dropped Bingo, and they both dived back through the door.

It didn't take long for Lennie to hand out a white handkerchief of surrender. In moments he and Eli were in police custody, hiding their faces from the glare of TV cameras as they were led into squad cars.

Bingo felt himself being swept up into the arms of the girl whose life he had saved. He felt himself being smothered by hugs — first hers, then her sister's. He felt camera lights bearing down on him like the desert sun. Behind him and the girls, the mother and father were grinning into the camera.

". . . And the Thompson family credit this remarkable dog with saving their lives," a reporter said into a mike. Then, turning to the father, he asked, "What are your plans now, Mr. Thompson?"

"We still have a few days' vacation left," Mr. Thompson said, "but we're going back to dogproof our house so we can give this little fella the best home he's ever had."

The best home he's ever had?

Chuckie gawked at the motel TV. It *had* to be Bingo; there was no mistaking that face. The poor thing was being smothered by the two girls, whose sickly sweet smiles reminded him of Star Search contestants. How could they be his new owners? Bingo could *never* be happy with them.

Chuckie fell to his knees. He could feel his heart sinking like a lead weight. There was absolutely nothing he could do. The best friend he ever had was about to become . . . a Thompson.

An agonized cry welled up from within Chuckie and shook the motel walls: "Bingoooo!"

He pressed his hand to the TV, as if Bingo could somehow feel him.

At that exact moment, to Chuckie's astonishment, Bingo turned and raised his paw to the camera himself.

Maybe it was a coincidence, but Chuckie didn't think so. He knew he was still somehow *connected* to Bingo. He always would be, no matter what dorky family called itself his owner.

Sure, they would have him in their house, Chuckie thought. I'll have him in my *soul*.

But as Chuckie turned off the TV, he couldn't stop himself from bursting into tears.

Chapter 11

Bingo the Dog
c/o The Thompson Family
c/o KYAP Television
Channel 9
Smokestack, Indiana

Honk! Honnnnk!

Chuckie quickly sealed his letter. Outside, his dad leaned on the car horn.

Stepping over the broken glass still left over from his dad's field goal attempt, Chuckie ran out the door. He rushed over to a mailbox just outside the motel office and dropped the letter inside. "I haven't forgotten you, pal," he whispered, imagining the letter in Bingo's paws. "Don't give up. You'll find me."

"Hey!" an irate voice called out. "What happened in here, a demolition derby?"

Chuckie looked over his shoulder to see the motel manager standing in the doorway of the Devlins' room. In his left hand he was holding a broken lamp, yet another victim of a Hal Devlin kick.

Chuckie practically flew into the station wagon.

"Wait a minute!" the manager shouted. "Who's going to pay for this?"

"Bill it to the Broncos!" Mr. Devlin called out through his window.

He pressed the accelerator so hard, it nearly went through the car floor. With a squeal of tires and a spray of gravel, the station wagon peeled out into the street.

Bingo hated the dress — but it was the frilly bonnet that *really* got him. It kept drooping over his eyes and pulling on his fur. Then there was the bedroom, all done up in pink, with hearts and pictures of rosy-cheeked teen idols on the walls.

He squirmed uncomfortably in the baby stroller Sandy Thompson had put him in. Was this the reward he got for saving the girl's *life*?

Who did these Thompson girls think he was?

Cindy Thompson burst into the room, looking around. "What have you done with Eugene?" she cried.

"You mean *Cuddles*?" answered Sandy.

"You call him what you want," Cindy said defiantly, "but his name is Eugene."

"Cuddles!"

"Eugene!"

Bingo wanted to throw up. Instead, he let out a frustrated yowl.

"Not again!" Cindy said, finally seeing Bingo in the stroller. "You know he hates playing baby!"

"He's my dog, too," Sandy protested. "You don't get him *all* the time."

The argument ended when Mr. Thompson walked in. "Uh, you'll both have to wait to play with him," he said.

A plain-looking man in a plain-looking suit stepped out from behind Mr. Thompson. He stared at Bingo and pulled a folded piece of paper out of his pocket. "You Bingo?" he asked.

"Rowf!" Bingo barked.

The man stuck the paper in Bingo's mouth. "It's a subpoena," he said.

"Girls," Mr. Thompson explained, "that means your dog has to go to court."

Bingo was happy to be out of his little-girl prison. But he never expected to end up on the witness stand of a court, taking an oath on a Bible.

It was a quiet room, with an old, bored-looking judge sitting behind a high desk. A bunch of people were staring at Bingo from the defense table, among them Lennie and Eli.

"Do you swear to tell the whole truth and nothing but the truth, so help you God?" a grim-faced man asked Bingo.

"Rowf!" Bingo barked.

Lennie and Eli's lawyer leapt up from the table. "Your Honor, I object!" he thundered. "This is a court of law, not a kennel!"

"Overruled!" the judge retorted. "Didn't you ever have a dog when you were a kid? Proceed, prosecutor."

The prosecutor nodded. He was the lawyer trying to send Lennie and Eli to jail. Turning to Bingo, he said, "Were you present on the night when the Thompson camper was hijacked by two ruthless armored-car thieves who held the family captive until the following morning?"

"Rowf! Rowf! Rowf-rowf-rowf!"

"Are those two thieves in the courtroom?" the prosecutor asked.

"Rowf!"

"Would you identify them for us?"

Bingo jumped over the witness-stand rail and ran to the defense. "Grrrrrr . . ." he growled, pointing to them like a hunting dog.

"Traitor!" Lennie said under his breath.

"Better keep the lights on," Eli said. "I'm going to get you!"

Smiling confidently, the prosecutor said, "No further questions, Your Honor."

Just then the defense attorney stood up. "I would like to cross-examine the witness!" Strolling toward the witness stand, he said, "Now, you indicated you were in the Thompsons' camper, but you didn't indicate *why* you were there. Can you tell the court where you were during the armored-car robbery earlier that day?"

"Objection, Your Honor!" the prosecutor bellowed. "That's irrelevant!"

"Your Honor, I have witnesses who will testify to seeing this dog near a trash can just before the robbery." He picked a small plaster shape off his table and handed it to the judge. "We would also like to introduce Exhibit Q, a cast of paw prints that substantiate he was at the scene of the crime."

"Wait just one minute!" the prosecutor said.

But the defense attorney just whirled around to Bingo and said, "Isn't it true *you* were the one who robbed the Fargo armored car? And didn't you subsequently frame my clients in a clever scheme to earn you wealth, respect, and a room of your own?"

A low murmur of surprise swept the courtroom. The prosecutor pounded the table, yelling, "Objection! The witness is not on trial here!"

"We contend there is a reasonable suspicion," the defense attorney barreled on, "and unless the witness has an alibi as to his whereabouts during the robbery, he should be bound over until contrary evidence is brought forth."

Bingo had no idea *what* he was talking about, but it didn't look good.

"Please answer the question," the judge said to Bingo. "Do you have an alibi?"

"Don't answer!" the prosecutor snapped. "You have rights."

"Answer, or I'll throw you in the slammer for contempt of court!" the judge said.

Bingo looked helplessly from one to the other. All he could manage was a tiny, confused whimper.

The judge smacked his gavel. "Take him away!"

The next few hours passed in a blur. But when they were over, Bingo was sharing a prison cell with a small, spectacled convict known only as Foureyes.

Bingo tried to look on the bright side. They *could*

have put him in with someone like Lennie or Eli or Duke, but they didn't. Foureyes seemed like a nice guy — and smart, too.

Especially when he lifted a couple of loose tiles from the cell floor, revealing a hole underneath.

Bingo wagged his tail, and Foureyes gave him a big smile. "Think you can help with my project?" he asked.

Within minutes Bingo was burrowing deep into the dirt below the prison. Foureyes used a mirror to keep watch of the hallway. Every few minutes he looked back at Bingo.

"Hey, you're really good!" he said as Bingo's tail slowly disappeared into the hole. "Have you done this before?"

A sudden whistle from down the hall made Foureyes hold out his mirror. He squinted at it, then quickly stuffed it in his pocket. "Someone's coming!" he whispered urgently to Bingo.

Bingo climbed out, and Foureyes quickly replaced the tiles. They scrambled over to a table and sat down. With blinding speed, Foureyes shuffled a deck of cards and handed some to Bingo. They fanned them and held them up, pretending to be playing.

The guard's footsteps got closer, then stopped in front of Bingo's cell. "You got mail," he announced.

Foureyes looked up from his cards. "It's about time."

"Not you," the guard said with a sneer. He jerked his head toward Bingo. "You."

Bingo barked happily. He dropped his cards and scampered to the door.

But the guard just grinned and held back the envelope. "*After* work," he said.

Bingo's spirits sank.

"It's okay, pal," Foureyes said. "That just means we have to do the prison laundry."

The guard led them to a huge room filled with washing machines. After Foureyes and Bingo stuck four enormous bins' worth of clothing into the machines, the guard finally put the letter in Bingo's mouth.

Whimpering, Bingo held the letter out to Foureyes.

"All right, I'll read it to you," Foureyes said, taking the letter. He opened it, pulled out a hand-written sheet of loose-leaf paper, and began to read. "Says here: 'Dear Bingo, I'm writing so you'll know I still think of you as my dog and I want you to find me so we can resume our happy life together. I saw those Thompson girls on the tube, and if you ask me, they look like real dodo birds. So I am asking you to blow them off, even if it is a semi-happy home, and pick up my trail, which I know you were following, because I have faith that you know I am the perfect kid for you, because I am lonely and picked-on like you.' "

Foureyes shook his head and muttered, "Who taught this kid English?"

"Rowf!" Bingo barked impatiently. It had to be Chuckie — but where was he? *Where was he?*

" 'Anyway,' " Foureyes continued reading, " 'if

you do this and find me, we will finally be happy, which I know you will like. See you soon, I hope. Your best friend, Chuckie. P.S. I forgot to tell you where I am, which I better do now, 'cause knowing you, you'll sniff this letter and try to retrace its delivery cross-country to where I mailed it from (ha! ha!). Anyway, all you have to do is get yourself to — ' "

Foureyes turned the letter to the other side. Bingo's heart was pumping like a machine gun.

But before Foureyes could read the other side, a hand reached over his shoulder and ripped the letter away!

Bingo looked up to see the leering faces of his old friends Lennie and Eli. "Lie down with dogs, and you wake up with fleas," Lennie said, holding the letter and grinning.

Foureyes stood up gallantly, his fists clenched. But his eyes only reached to Lennie's chest, so he moved over to face Eli instead. "You talking to *me*?" he asked.

"No," Eli replied. "We're talking to that good-for-nothing, back-stabbing, double-crossing hair wad you're with."

Then, with a lightning-quick move, Foureyes reached out and grabbed the letter.

Lennie's grip tightened. With a loud rip, the letter tore in half.

"Let's have the rest of it!" Foureyes demanded.

Lennie crumpled up his half of the letter — the half with Chuckie's address on it. Bingo barked desperately.

Then, as if he were eating candy, Lennie popped his half of the letter in his mouth and began to chew. With his cheeks puffed, and his mouth twisted into an evil smile, he said, "Come and get it!"

With that, he pulled out a gleaming, homemade knife.

Chapter 12

Eli pulled out an even bigger homemade knife.

Other inmates in the laundry room circled around. *They* pulled out homemade knives.

The inmates circled around Lennie and Eli. Lennie and Eli circled around Foureyes. Foureyes circled around Bingo.

And Bingo started barking like crazy.

A guard came barging into the room. "Hey, who's doing all that barking?" he shouted.

Instantly the knives disappeared into the inmates' pockets.

The guard stepped into the middle of the crowd, looking around suspiciously. "If that's the way you want to play it," he said, "back to your cells!"

As he began pushing the inmates toward the door, Lennie leaned toward Bingo and mumbled, "You're dog meat, pal."

"It ain't over till it's over," Eli added.

Bingo hung his head. It *was* over, but not the way Eli thought. Bingo's entire reason for living was over. Chuckie's address was traveling down some sleazy crook's esophagus, and Bingo would never find out what it was.

When they got back to the jail cell, Bingo threw himself into his digging. If he couldn't have Chuckie, at least he could try to get out of prison.

Just before sundown, he broke through to the other side. But the chances of escaping safely would be greatest in the darkness, so he and Foureyes waited.

After all that digging, Bingo was tired. He dozed off, until Foureyes jabbed him at about three A.M.

"It's time," Foureyes whispered. "There's only one tower guard, and he's at the end of his shift. He'll be tired and bored. Let's go."

Quickly, silently, they both wriggled into the tunnel and crawled under the cell-block wall. Foureyes carried a long rope that was tied to the wooden seat he'd taken from his toilet.

They emerged into the prison yard. Around them, searchlights swept back and forth. Staying close to the ground, Foureyes scrambled across the yard, with Bingo close behind. They dodged the lights left and right, lurching toward the prison wall.

At the base of the wall, Foureyes boosted Bingo up and over. Bingo landed on the other side with a soft thud.

Foureyes checked the rope to make sure it was tied tightly to the toilet seat. Then he tossed the seat over the wall, holding his end of the rope.

Bingo grabbed the seat with his teeth and slipped

his head into it. Using it as a harness, he pulled with all his might.

Foureyes felt his feet lift off the ground. Slowly he rose up the wall. It was working! Bingo was strong enough! Foureyes tingled with joy.

Until he looked upward.

He hadn't thought about the barbed wire. He hadn't even seen it in the darkness. But there it was, sharp and rusty, just waiting for him at the top of the wall. Foureyes gritted his teeth. He closed his eyes. . . .

"YEEEEEEEEOUCHHH!"

Up in the watchtower, the guard bolted from his seat. He slapped down the magazine he'd been reading and grabbed his rifle. Taking a flashlight with his other hand, he stepped out of the tower and onto a catwalk.

"Darn rifle is so heavy. . . ." he muttered to himself. He stuck the flashlight in his mouth and held his rifle with both arms. Jerking his head left and right, he sent the light on a jagged path around the area just over the wall.

Below, huddled against the wall, Bingo licked the cuts on Foureyes's face. The light jumped around crazily, just missing them.

"Don't worry about me, boy, I just need a little after-shave," Foureyes whispered. He quickly took the torn piece of Chuckie's letter out of his pocket. Then he held it up and let Bingo sniff it. "I hope you know what you're doing," he said, tucking the letter into Bingo's collar. "The post office isn't much for direct routes — but I guess you'll do all right, you lucky son-of-a-gun!"

Bingo licked him on the cheek, and Foureyes smiled. "I'll never forget you."

The two of them sneaked away in opposite directions, and Bingo could hear Foureyes singing softly, "There was a con who had a dog and Bingo was his name-o. B-I-N — "

Crackk! Crackk!

Two bullets hit a tree directly in front of Foureyes. "Halt!" the guard shouted — but when he did, the flashlight tumbled out of his mouth.

Bingo and Foureyes peeled out. And as the guard sent a hailstorm of wild gunfire around them, they escaped into the woods.

It didn't take Bingo long to find the nearest post office. The place was small and dumpy, but Bingo was trembling with excitement. The scent was there, the scent from Chuckie's letter — he *knew* it.

He sniffed around trucks and stacks of mailbags. Finally, near the loading-dock entrance, he found it — strong and clear, and leading up the road to the right.

With a howl of triumph, he started on his trail.

Chuckie liked Green Bay all right. The weather was warmer, the land flatter, the people talked in a weird accent and ate a lot of meat. The house was bigger than the Denver house — which made it feel that much more empty without Bingo.

On a Saturday morning, he and Chickie played a video game in the living room. Their mom was sitting on the couch with a racing form, and their dad was reading the sports section. The headline blared out, in big bold letters, CAN DEVLIN DO IT? KICKING GAME KEY TO PACKER PLAY-OFF HOPES.

Suddenly Mr. Devlin lowered the paper. His face was as white as a sheet. He stared at his kicking foot, which was propped up on a soft ottoman.

"What is it, Hal?" Mrs. Devlin asked.

Her husband wiggled his toes. "It's tingling — like it used to. Remember?"

"What on earth . . . ?" Mrs. Devlin said, her voice trailing off.

Mr. Devlin brought his foot inward. With both hands, he brought it close to his face and inspected it carefully. Chuckie turned to look.

"I'd forgotten what it felt like, Natalie," Mr. Devlin said, his voice choked with emotion. "The touch — I think it's coming back! I think the old foot is finally waking up!"

Chuckie smiled. He knew why his dad's foot was coming to life. The air was charged with excitement — he could feel it. And that could mean only one thing.

"Bingo," he whispered. "He's on his way! He must be!" He spun around to face Chickie. "I knew it! I told you he'd come!"

Days passed, then weeks. Bingo followed the trail of Chuckie's letter faithfully, however he could. He hopped jeeps, stowed away on trucks and planes, jumped on trains. He waded through rivers, staggered through deserts, got drenched in rainstorms. Utah, Oregon, Wyoming, South Dakota, Illinois, Michigan, Kentucky, Kansas — all of them were names he saw on road signs.

As he passed a boxy-looking motel, somewhere in Indiana, he was beginning to think he'd never find Chuckie. Could this whole thing be a mistake?

Then the trail stopped.

At least it seemed that way. Bingo backtracked and sniffed again. He was right about one thing. The trail *had* stopped moving along the street. But it seemed to lead toward the motel.

He followed the scent as far as it went — to the motel mailbox.

This was it! This was where Chuckie mailed the letter! It wasn't the kind of place he'd expected the Devlins to be living, but then again, he never really understood humans' tastes.

Bingo wanted to let out a victorious howl, but what came out was hoarse and pinched. The long journey had taken its toll. Bingo had kept himself going with the hope of seeing Chuckie — and now that he reached his goal, his body was shutting down.

Bingo put his nose to the ground again. It was getting so that he could smell nothing *but* Chuckie, he thought. Everything else — flowers, food, even garbage — seemed to have no odor.

None of it mattered. In minutes he would be in Chuckie's strong arms. Chuckie would know how to make him feel better.

Bingo picked up a faint Chuckie scent, leading to a motel-room door. With his last ounce of strength, he gave the door a few weak scratches.

The door swung open. Bingo felt a surge of new energy. His tail wagged for the first time since the prison break.

Then, as fast as his energy had come, it disappeared. It wasn't Chuckie in the doorway. It wasn't any of the Devlins.

A woman stared down at him. Her hair was fiery-red, and she was wearing makeup so thick it looked like a mask. "Awww," she said. "It's a cute doggy!" She knelt down to pick him up.

And that was when Bingo passed out.

When he woke up, he was in a room with white walls. A man with a white uniform was giving instructions to a younger man and woman, both wearing white. Bingo began to whine. He tried to get up, but his legs were tied down.

"Easy, honey," a voice reassured him. He looked up to see the red-haired woman. "It's me, Bunny," she said. "Everything's going to be all right. You're at Dr. Frick's office. He's a vet."

Bingo looked at Dr. Frick. He was putting on rubber gloves. "You have the smell receptors for the transplant?" he asked his assistant.

"In here," the assistant answered, holding up a thick, plastic ice chest. "They're from a Doberman."

"Doberman?" the doctor repeated.

The assistant shrugged. "Best I could do."

"Well, we have no choice," Dr. Frick said. "Without a transplant, his sense of smell is shot. He's overworked his own nose, and his nasal membrane looks like a worn-out shoe. I just hope we're not too late." He cracked his knuckles and wrung out his arms nervously. "Okay, knock him out and let's slap those babies in his schnozz."

Doberman? Smell-receptor transplant? Bingo couldn't believe what he was hearing.

As the assistant lowered a small gas mask to his face, Bingo struggled with his remaining strength.

"Don't worry, boy," the assistant said. "Doc's the best. Just count to ten backward. . . ."

Bingo felt the mask smothering him. Trembling, he started to count.

He hadn't even reached seven when everything faded to black.

Chapter 13

"Bingo! *Bingoooooo!*"

Chuckie's voice echoed in the school corridor. He knew Bingo was there, somewhere. He also knew something was terribly, terribly wrong.

He blinked, squeezing the tears out of his eyes. Then, in a thin voice, cracked and breaking with sadness, he began to sing: "Th-there was a kid who had . . . a dog, and Bingo was his name-o. B-I-N — "

He waited, but there was no answer.

"I know you're here, boy!" Chuckie called out. "Say something! *Do* something!"

"Do you have a pass, young man?" a nasal voice interrupted from behind him.

Chuckie turned to see Mrs. Grimbleby approaching. She was his least-favorite teacher — with a face like Freddy Krueger, and a personality like the Wicked Witch of the West.

"Aren't you supposed to be in biology, Chickie?" Mrs. Grimbleby demanded.

"No, I'm Chuckie."

"Don't sass me, young man. Your pass?"

"I — I don't have one . . . but I heard my dog and — "

Mrs. Grimbleby's eyes narrowed. "Dog? What dog?"

"*Rowf! Rowf!*"

There it was! The bark was muffled and metallic, as if Bingo were inside one of the lockers.

Chuckie ran from Mrs. Grimbleby. "Bingo!" he shouted, yanking open the lockers along the hall.

With superhuman speed he looked in all of them, and all of them were empty. The barking continued, louder and louder, until there was just one closed locker left.

That was when Mrs. Grimbleby finally grabbed him.

"*Rowf! Rowf!*" The barking was growing frantic.

"No!" Chuckie screamed, trying to break away from Mrs. Grimbleby's iron grip. "He's my dog!"

Mrs. Grimbleby pressed her warty face against his. "You're in very serious trouble, young man. You'll be twenty-five years old before you graduate from here!"

Chuckie did the first thing that came to mind — he bit her nose. As she screamed and fell back, he reached for the last locker and pulled it open.

What he saw made him turn chalk-white. It wiped the smile off his face and made his knees weak.

It was Bingo, all right. But in the middle of his face was the long, pointed, black snout of a Doberman!

* * *

"NOOOOOOOOOOO!"

Chuckie bolted upright in his bed. His football posters came into focus, then his video-game boxes and magazines. He was home.

It was a dream . . . it was a dream . . . he kept repeating to himself. But his heart was beating like a jackhammer, and his forehead was covered with sweat. It seemed so real.

So real.

His door opened, and his mom peered in. "You all right, son?"

"Nightmare, that's all," Chuckie said.

She came in and kissed his forehead gently. "No more horror videos before bed, okay?"

Chuckie nodded, still numb. She was right, the video must have been what caused it. It couldn't have been anything else.

Still, as he tried to go back to sleep, he wasn't sure. . . .

A week later, in Bunny's motel room in Smokestack, Indiana, Dr. Frick began unwrapping bandages from Bingo's nose. "His sense of smell will need plenty of stimulation," he explained. "See if he responds to familiar foods and people . . . ah, here we are!"

With a gentle flourish, he pulled the last bandage off. Bunny gasped and shrank away in horror. Bingo's eyes filled with concern.

"Just kidding," Bunny said with a sudden smile.

Dr. Frick spun Bingo around so he was facing a

85

mirror. His nose was as good as new!

As Bingo barked with happiness, Bunny and Dr. Frick applauded. "Now," the doctor said, "let's see how that old sniffer's working."

He pulled out a deck of cards. "Let me teach you to play a little three-card monte," he said to Bingo. He peeled off three cards, including the Queen of Spades. "Now I'll give the Queen my own personal scent," he said, rubbing the card on his face.

He put the Queen facedown on the bed, next to the other two cards. Then he picked them up, stacked them, put them down again, and began moving them around. "Watch the Queen," Dr. Frick said. "She moves, she grooves, she's here, she's there, under, over, this way, that . . ."

Finally he stopped. The three cards were lined up facedown, looking identical. "Okay, fella," he said to Bingo. "Pick the Queen."

Bunny stared at the cards, baffled. Bingo leaned over them and carefully sniffed each one. Then he put his paw on the card in the middle.

Dr. Frick flipped it over to reveal the Queen of Spades. "Congratulations," he said. "The operation was a success!"

"I could have sworn it was the one on the left," Bunny said.

"That's because you're using your eyes, not your nose," the doctor said with a confident smile. "Now, about my bill . . ."

After seeing how much Dr. Frick charged, Bunny needed a new source of income — and with

Bingo, she found it. She took him to city street corners, where con artists were playing three-card monte games. She would pretend not to know how to play, then pick up the Queen and rub it between her fingers to give it her scent. When she put it back, Bingo was on the alert.

For days, they never lost a game. Bunny packed away stacks of twenty-dollar bills in her motel room.

Bunny was thrilled, but Bingo never enjoyed it. Day by day, he grew quieter and less energetic. He tried not to show it. After all, he owed Bunny his sense of smell — maybe his life. And she *was* a nice person. The least he could do was be a good dog for her.

But still, she wasn't Chuckie, and it was hard for Bingo to hide his sadness. One rainy evening, he and Bunny sat in the motel room, silently looking out the window.

Suddenly Bunny picked a rubber ball off the floor. "Hey! You want to play ball?"

She threw the ball across the room. It bounced off the opposite wall and careened wildly around.

Bingo's eyes followed the ball briefly, then looked back outside, imagining how far away Chuckie might really be.

"How about a chew stick?" Bunny asked. "A squeaky toy? Raw meat?"

Bingo didn't even move.

Bunny walked over and sat next to him. "What's the matter? You don't fetch, play, nip at my heels, get the paper, water the plants, bark at strangers. . . . I want a pet, not a doorstop!" She sighed, and her voice became softer. "You miss Chuckie, don't you?"

Bingo snapped right around and looked her in the eye. How did *she* know about Chuckie?

"I read the letter," Bunny said. "What was left of it, anyway."

She got up and walked to her dresser. "You came here looking for Chuckie, didn't you?" she said. "You tracked him this far, but the rest of the letter was ripped . . ."

Pulling Chuckie's crumpled letter from the top drawer, she gave Bingo a sad smile. "I was hoping you'd forget — that maybe you'd want to be *my* dog. But I know now I can't compete with this Chuckie. And I can't hold you against your will forever."

Bingo whimpered, his eyes bright with hope.

"How should I know where he is?" Bunny said. "Finding him is your problem."

He snuggled next to her, putting his head on her lap. All Bunny's defenses instantly melted away. "Oh, all right. I'll try to find out."

She left the room and was gone for a half hour. When she came back, her face was set with determination. "Get ready. We're going to the bus station."

Bunny raced over to the kitchenette. With a flurry of activity, she began pulling things from her refrigerator, then preparing some food. Then she reached into her dresser and took out a shoebox decorated with sequins and pictures of dogs. "Like it?" she said. "I made it for you one night while you were sleeping."

One good thing about being a dog is you can't say what's on your mind. The word *gross* was on Bingo's mind. But he wagged his tail, and that made Bunny happy. She began stuffing things into the box left and right.

She didn't tell him what she had found out, or where he was going, until they were at the bus station. Bingo realized it was because she didn't want to dwell on it; she was afraid she'd start crying.

Finally, on a waiting-room bench, she said, "The motel man told me they were headed for Green Bay, Wisconsin. The bus will get you there, but then you're on your own. Find that little boy and start your life again. I'll be fine."

Her eyes began to water. "I've knitted you a tail warmer," she said, pulling out a horrible-looking wool cylinder from the shoebox. "And I've packed you some other travel goodies — dog biscuits, a puzzle, magazines. And some cold-cream-and-jelly sandwiches. Your favorite."

"*All aboard for Green Bay!*" a voice squawked over the station loudspeaker.

"You crazy mutt!" Bunny said, giving Bingo a big hug. "I guess I didn't know what real love was until you came along."

With that, she put him on the bus.

Bingo jumped into a seat and looked out a window. As the bus pulled away, he could see her mascara running down her face as she cried.

He felt sad, too, but his mood began to lift quickly. The sign on the bus had said GREEN BAY. And every block they traveled was a block closer to Chuckie.

Bingo had finished the contents of the shoebox by the next bus stop. He left the box in a station trash can, feeling a little pang of guilt.

When the bus left the station, he quickly forgot about it. And so did the trash collector that night.

It was still lying there the next morning when a bloodhound began sniffing it and howling wildly.

There were two men with him. The taller of the two yanked the dog back, and the other pulled a piece of wax paper out of the box and tasted the white-and-purple food that was smudged on it.

"What is it?" the taller one asked.

"Cold cream and jelly," the shorter one answered.

Eli smiled at Lennie. They were getting closer.

Chapter 14

Bingo read the bus station sign over and over:

WELCOME TO GREEN BAY
HOME OF THE PACKERS

He could barely control his excitement. He stepped over laps and between legs, hurrying to the front of the bus.

When he got off, he went right to work. He sniffed the ground, the walls, the sidewalks.

Nothing.

He ran to a nearby tavern. There was a phone booth near the cashier, with a phone book on a shelf underneath. Taking the book in his mouth, he climbed a bar stool and sat down. Then he put the book down on the bar and began looking for the *D* section.

All around him, people were staring, some with their mouths hanging open. But Bingo didn't notice a thing. His eyes were scanning a page in the book:

Dennison . . . Department of health . . . Destry . . . Deutschman . . . Devaron . . .

There it was, in black and white:

Devlin, H.   1801 Filbert Court   555–3370

The book had a foldout map of Green Bay in the back. Bingo pulled it open, located Filbert Court, and raced out of the bar.

It took him three minutes to get across town. As he turned onto Filbert, he noticed the maples and oaks, the perfect lawns, the sturdy fire hydrants.

It would be a perfect place to live, he thought.

Then he saw them. Chuckie's mom and dad. He almost squealed with pleasure, but held his tongue. If *they* saw him, he might never have the chance to see Chuckie.

He waited patiently behind a neighbor's hedge.

Mr. Devlin kissed his wife on the front porch and walked to his car.

"Give it to Detroit, dear!" Mrs. Devlin called to him. "Make those play-offs!"

Mr. Devlin winked at her, then got in the car and backed out of the driveway. Bingo's wary eyes followed the station wagon down the street, one block . . . two blocks. . . .

And that was when he caught sight of Chuckie. Or Chuckie's head, to be exact, bobbing up and down above a hedge about two blocks away. As Mr. Devlin passed his son, he honked and waved.

Bingo was so deliriously happy, he could hardly move. Then he began running so fast, he nearly fell over his own feet. His eyes stayed glued to Chuckie. It wasn't a dream, he told himself. It wasn't mistaken identity. The walk, the scent, the way the hair bounced — it was all genuine Chuckie Devlin!

His tongue hung out with the effort of running. He pulled it back in, preparing to unleash a howl of unbelievable joy.

But right then, Chuckie walked past the hedge — and Bingo stopped short.

The howl caught in his throat. He couldn't even bark. Couldn't move an inch. He felt as if his feet were glued to the street.

Chuckie had a leash in his hand. The leash was attached to a dog. Both of them were walking along, looking happy as could be.

Another dog.

Chuckie had another dog.

The words pounded Bingo's brain like a hammer on an anvil. The idea of it chilled him to the soul. He'd expected Chuckie to have made new friends, pick up new hobbies — maybe even get a fish, like his parents had suggested. But a new dog? It had never entered his mind.

Unspeakable horror settled over him like a smothering blanket. When he thought about it, it made perfect sense. Why *shouldn't* Chuckie have a dog? Chuckie deserved happiness. It would be selfish for Bingo to assume that Chuckie would just wait forever, lonely and miserable.

Bingo's head drooped low. He slowly turned around and slinked down the street.

Had he paid attention a few moments longer, he

would have seen Chuckie walk the dog up a neighbor's front steps and ring the bell. He would have seen a woman answer the door, give Chuckie a dollar bill, and say, "Here you go, Chuckie. It was nice of you to walk Frisker for me."

And he would have seen Chuckie walk back to his own house, dogless but with thoughts of Bingo in his head.

As it was, Bingo wandered aimlessly through the Green Bay streets for hours. It wasn't until he passed a restaurant that he realized he hadn't eaten since Bunny's cold-cream-and-jelly sandwiches. His stomach was growling with hunger.

The restaurant was called Vic's Café, and it was crowded. To Bingo, that meant there would be *lots* of food scraps.

He sneaked around back and turned over a garbage can. It clattered to the ground with a huge crash, spilling out half-eaten portions of prime rib and veal chops — and bringing the restaurant owner on the run.

The man picked up Bingo by the scruff of his neck and looked him in the eye. "You're new around here, ain't you?" he said. "Well, I don't care how pathetic you are — if you want food from ol' Vic, you have to earn your money!"

The next thing Bingo knew, he was in the kitchen with a white cap on his head. Beside him stood a skinny, scared-looking teenager. Vic left for a moment, then came back with a pile of dirty dishes. He plopped them on a counter in front of Bingo and said, "I'll have more when you finish with these. Dave here will show you the ropes."

Without saying a word, Dave slipped on a pair of rubber gloves and took the top plate off the stack. Bingo expected him to turn on the water and wash it, but he didn't. Instead he held the plate to Bingo's mouth.

Bingo looked at him, puzzled. Then it dawned on him: He was supposed to *lick* it clean!

It seemed like a strange way to do dishes, but Bingo didn't mind it a bit.

"Saves on our water bill!" Vic said with a laugh. Then he leaned in toward Dave. "Better stay on your toes. This mutt looks ambitious."

Dave's face grew tense and worried, as if he was afraid Bingo was going to steal his job away. He handed plate after plate to Bingo, secretly hoping Bingo would leave a small scrap, a tiny stain of food.

But Bingo was hungry — and the food was good. He licked every plate spotless. It wasn't making the thought of Chuckie go away, but it sure was easing the pain.

The next day, Lennie and Eli walked up to a telephone pole with a stack of posters. Their bloodhound padded along beside them. "I hope this is the right place," Lennie said.

"Green Bay, that's what the guy at the bus station said," Eli replied, tacking one of the posters to the pole. " 'The pooch with the shoebox was on a bus to Green Bay.' Those were his exact words."

He stepped back and looked at the poster. In the

center was a crude drawing of Bingo. Above it, in big letters, was the message LOST DOG — $500 REWARD. Below the picture it said, *If you have any information leading to our dog, Bingo, contact Room 12 at the Highway Motor Inn. Ask for Mr. Smith.*

"I don't know," Lennie said. "Five hundred bucks is a lot for a reward."

Eli rolled his eyes. "Who says we're going to pay up?"

"You mean, we don't pay up?" Lennie asked.

"We're *crooks*, Lennie. We don't have to pay up. Now quit your bellyaching. We've got a lot of ground to cover."

By the end of the day, they had plastered the whole town of Green Bay with signs. Then they trudged back to their motel room and had lunch.

As Lennie stood in the bathroom, brushing his teeth, he heard a knock at the door. He opened it and came face to face with Dave, the teenager from Vic's Café.

"Yeah?" Lennie said. "What do you want, pal?"

"You Mr. Smith?" Dave asked timidly.

Lennie scrunched his brow with confusion and called over his shoulder, "Eli! Is there a Mr. Smith here?"

Eli ran over from the kitchen area and elbowed Lennie in the rib cage. "We're Mr. Smith," he blurted to Dave.

"Um, well, I think the dog you're looking for is working at Vic's Café as the assistant dishwasher." He made sure to emphasize the word *assistant*.

"You sure?" Eli said.

Dave nodded. "He ain't been promoted *yet*."

"Come on, Lennie!" Eli shouted. "You, too, Ol' Blue!"

The bloodhound, who had been napping on the floor, stood up instantly.

Lennie picked up Ol' Blue's leash and put it in Dave's hand. "Hold this," he said, as he and Eli rushed out the door.

Completely befuddled, Dave shouted after them, "Hey, what about my reward?"

Lennie and Eli hopped into a blue Chevy and slammed the doors. "Sell Ol' Blue!" Lennie replied.

The Chevy's tires left dark black skid marks as it roared down the street. His face red with anger and embarrassment, Dave picked up some rocks and threw them after the car.

He paid no attention to Chuckie Devlin, who was on the road, pedaling madly toward the motel, his Packer cap pushed tightly over his head. Chuckie had biked as fast as he could, as soon as he'd seen the poster. He hadn't expected to be in the line of fire of a crazed rock-thrower with a bloodhound.

"Hey, what's going on here?" Chuckie shouted.

Dave watched the Chevy speed away, then looked at Chuckie. His face grew red, and his eyes darted about nervously, as if he couldn't figure out what to say.

Then, finally, he held up Ol' Blue's leash. "Um, you want to buy a dog?"

Chapter 15

"You're a hard worker, Bingo," Vic said as Bingo left the restaurant that evening. "I like that. You be here at six tomorrow and we'll talk more about career opportunities in the food-service industry."

Bingo stepped out of the kitchen and into the alleyway. Maybe Vic's Café was his destiny, he thought. He had to make *something* of his life, post-Chuckie.

Suddenly, he couldn't breathe. There was something around his neck. He struggled, but it got tighter.

Out of the shadows came Lennie. In his right arm was a long stick with a rope attached to it — the rope that he had managed to loop around Bingo's neck.

Lennie's voice was a ghostly rasp. "Well, if it ain't Mr. Whole-truth-and-nothing-but-the-truth-flea-carrying-turncoat-snitch!"

Then Eli emerged from the darkness, his craggy face a mask of terror in the faint light. "Before we're finished," he said, "you're going to wish you'd never been whelped!"

Shhhhheeeeeeeee!

All three of them turned toward the sidewalk. Chuckie was skidding into the alleyway on his bike. Without losing his balance, he pedaled toward Lennie. "Let go of my dog, you jerk!" he yelled.

Lennie tried to get out of the way, but the alley was too narrow. Chuckie smacked into him, full-force.

The bike thudded to the ground. Chuckie fell off. Lennie collapsed to the ground, clutching his side. Eli leapt on top of them, grabbing Chuckie's arms.

And Bingo wriggled free of his capture-stick.

"Run, Bingo! Run!" Chuckie yelled.

Eli lunged for Bingo, but not in time. Bingo was already at the sidewalk.

"Move it! Move it!" Eli screamed, pushing Chuckie and Lennie out of the alley. They all piled into the Chevy, which was parked by the curb.

And as they tore off into the night, Bingo watched them, hidden behind a stack of wooden boxes on the sidewalk.

The Chevy cruised through the dark and deserted Green Bay streets. Lennie and Eli stared left and right, looking for shadows in alleyways.

A wisp of putrid smoke rose from a cigar in Eli's mouth. "I'm losing my patience, boy," he said to Chuckie. "He's your dog. Now you're going to tell us where he is."

"How am I supposed to know?" Chuckie asked. "ESP?"

Eli puffed his cigar until the end of it glowed red. Then he took it out and held the lit end close to Chuckie's cheek. "Think real hard, wise guy."

"Y-y-you don't scare me," Chuckie said, lying. "When my dad gets wind of this, he'll beat the hair off you."

"Yeah?" Lennie said with a smile. "Him and who else?"

Chuckie sneered back at him. "How about the entire offensive line of the Green Bay Packers?"

Eli cackled. "Is that so? What is he, president of the booster club?"

"Try Hal Devlin," Chuckie said defiantly.

"Devlin, the placekicker?" Eli replied, his eyes wide.

Chuckie nodded with pride.

"He stunk up the stadium in Denver. Cost me some big dollars."

"Well, he's eight for eight with Green Bay, and we're going to make the play-offs after we hammer Detroit!"

Lennie burst into the conversation. "What is this, *NFL Today*? Both of you, shut up!"

"Wait a minute!" Eli said. His lips slowly turned up into a crooked grin. "How would you like to score some *real* money, Lennie?"

"What about the dog?" Lennie said. "We're after the dog!"

"*Forget the dog!*" Eli retorted. "This kid is our

passport to Fat City. We are going to make a bundle!"

As Eli talked about his plan, Chuckie listened with horror. It involved him, and it was not very pleasant.

Fortunately, Bingo was listening, too — sitting on top of the Chevy, safely out of sight, where he had quietly hopped just moments before.

He was hatching a plan of his own.

When the Chevy pulled into the parking lot of an old warehouse, Bingo jumped off and hid. Lennie and Eli pushed Chuckie inside the building. There was a lot of commotion, then silence. Cautiously, Bingo walked to the nearest warehouse window.

There was a pile of boxes under the window. Bingo climbed on it, stood on his hind legs, and looked inside.

At first he didn't see Chuckie. Huge, hulking metallic equipment stood in the middle of the warehouse like dinosaurs frozen in time. Along the walls were stacks of cardboard boxes that looked as if they hadn't been touched in years. One of the boxes was open, and Bingo could see leather suitcases inside. Shafts of light slanted in through the windows, and through a hole near the base of the back wall.

Off to one side was an inner office with a frosted-glass window. Inside it, Bingo could see the silhouettes of Lennie and Eli.

And then he saw Chuckie, sitting in a chair in

the warehouse, dwarfed by the machines that surrounded him. He was bound and gagged, and trying valiantly to break loose.

Bingo looked again at the hole in the back wall. It was his best hope of getting in.

He jumped off the boxes and ran around the warehouse, past a door that looked like it led into the inner office. He spotted the hole just past the door, and headed right for it.

But just as he got past the door, it flew open. Bingo hurled himself to the wall and crouched in a shadow.

Eli came storming out. "You hurry up with the explosives. I'll be right back after I find a phone and place this bet before kickoff."

"Yeah, but Eli," came Lennie's voice from inside the office, "everything we have on *one game*?"

"Lennie, it isn't gambling when you mark the deck. *You* worry about the kid and rigging the device."

With that, Eli walked out, leaving the door open. Bingo waited till he was out of sight, then looked in.

Lennie was hunched over a suitcase. From the way it looked, he must have stolen it from one of the warehouse boxes. But this suitcase was chock-full — with dynamite.

Lennie placed a small object inside. Bingo squinted and saw what looked like a digital clock on the object.

Standing back from the suitcase, Lennie pointed a black remote controller at it. When he clicked the remote controller, the digital clock began counting off. When he clicked it again, the clock stopped.

It was a timer, Bingo realized. A timer for the dynamite. But what was Lennie going to do with it?

The hair began to rise along Bingo's spine. A mixture of hate, anger, and fear coursed through him. He realized Chuckie was in trouble, and he was determined to do something about it.

Behind Lennie was the half-open door that led into the warehouse. Bingo waited until Lennie's back was turned, then stepped into the office.

Without a sound, he slipped past him and through the inner door.

Chuckie's eyes practically bugged out when he saw Bingo. "What are you doing here?" he said, his voice muffled by the gag in his mouth.

Bingo pawed the floor helplessly and whimpered. How could he possibly warn Chuckie about Lennie and Eli's terrible plot?

"Get help!" Chuckie said. "Go to my house. Get somebody — now!"

Bingo just stood there, not knowing what to do. He just *couldn't* leave Chuckie there all alone.

"*Now!*" Chuckie shouted.

Bingo backpedaled. Out of the corner of his eye, he saw the hole in the wall. He bolted for it, bumping into a ladder on the way.

WHHHHACCKKK! The ladder hit the ground with a sound that reverberated through the warehouse.

Chuckie went stiff. He heard Lennie scrambling

in the office. He saw Bingo furiously racing away.

Before Bingo could reach the hole, the office door slammed open. Lennie rushed in from the office. His face was red and tense.

When he spoke, his voice boomed through the warehouse like the voice of Doom itself. "*What* is going on in here?"

Chapter 16

Chuckie held his breath. Lennie was staring at *him*. Bingo had a chance of escaping, but only if Chuckie could provide a distraction for a few seconds.

But what?

There was no time to think. Chuckie did the first thing that came to mind. He began to sing. Loud. "There was a farmer had a dog and Bingo was his name-o . . ."

Lennie stared at him in disgust. "Shut up! I hate that song!"

As Lennie stalked back into the office, Chuckie's eyes darted right. Bingo was gone.

He slumped into his chair. It had worked. Now everything was up to Bingo.

Mrs. Devlin was making popcorn for the game when the doorbell rang. She wiped melted butter off her hand, ran to the door, and opened it.

It was Bingo, jumping and barking madly.

"Who are you?" she said. "We don't want any. Now get out of here. *Shoo! Shoo!*"

She slammed the door and ran back into the kitchen. The popcorn was ready, so she buttered it and put it in a bowl on a tray with other snacks. Then she took the tray into the living room and arranged everything neatly in front of the TV.

A while later, the doorbell rang again. "Chickieee!" she called out. "Will you get that?"

Chickie ran downstairs from his room and opened the door. It was Bingo again. He had gone back to the warehouse and taken Chuckie's Packer cap. Holding it in his teeth, he thrust it toward Chickie.

"Where'd you get this?" Chickie asked, taking the cap.

"Rowf!" Bingo barked.

"Just a minute," Chickie said suspiciously. He brought the cap into the living room.

"Who was it?" Mrs. Devlin asked.

"Some dog with a hat," Chickie said. "It looks like Chuckie's."

"Don't be silly. Do you know how many Packer caps there are in this town?"

Chickie nodded. He took the hat back to the door, threw it at Bingo, and slammed the door in his face.

A few minutes later, the phone rang. Mrs. Devlin ran inside the kitchen to answer it. "Hello?" she said.

The voice on the other end sounded as if it were underwater. She couldn't understand a word.

"Huh? Huh?" she said.

Rrrrrring! The doorbell again.

"Please, just a minute," she said into the phone. Covering the mouthpiece, she yelled, "Chickieeee!

The door!" Then she spoke back into the phone. "Could you enunciate more clearly? I'm having difficulty understanding you."

On the other end, at a roadside phone booth, Eli yanked a wad of cloth off the mouthpiece. He thought it would *disguise* his voice, not obliterate it. "I said, we've got your kid!" he shouted with exasperation.

At the same time, Chickie pulled the front door open to face Bingo again. This time Bingo was holding Chuckie's shirt. "You again?" Chickie said. "Get out of here before I call animal control!"

He slammed the door again, then went into the kitchen. His mom was hanging up the phone, her face ashen.

"What's wrong, Mom?" Chickie asked. "You look like you've seen a ghost."

Mrs. Devlin had a faraway look in her eyes. "Who was at the door?" she asked.

"That dumb dog again," Chickie said.

Mrs. Devlin bolted to the front door like a shot and flung it open. "Where is he?" she said, looking up and down the street.

"I chased him off."

"You've got to find him!"

"Why?"

"Someone's got Chuckie! That dog may know where he is!"

At the Detroit Silverdome, marching bands blared, cheerleaders screamed, and fans yelled at each other and the players. It was almost gametime.

On the sidelines, Hal Devlin took his pregame practice kicks, landing one after another perfectly into a net.

He felt better than he had in months. His field goals had won the last three games in the final minutes. Almost single-handedly he had brought the Packers from third place to a tie for first. And if they won this one, it was play-off time!

As he got ready for another practice kick, his coach tapped him on the shoulder pads. "It's for you," he said, handing him his headphones.

Mr. Devlin exhaled. He hated having his concentration broken before the game. "Yeah?" he said.

"Hal, it's me," came his wife's voice.

"I told you not to call me here," he snapped.

"They've got Chuckie!" Mrs. Devlin barreled on.

"Who's got Chuckie?"

"Kidnappers! They said that if we wanted to see him alive again — "

Mr. Devlin couldn't believe his ears. "Pay them! Understand? He's my son, for God's sake. We'll pay anything!"

"It's not exactly that kind of ransom." Mrs. Devlin swallowed hard. "They . . . well, they . . . they want . . ."

"Tell me!"

"They want you to miss your field goals!"

Mr. Devlin's jaw dropped open. "What?" His coach was gesturing toward him, pointing to his watch. Just beyond him, the entire Packer team was gathering in a pregame huddle. "Natalie, did they say anything about extra points?"

"No."

"Good. Listen carefully. Call the police and — "

The team huddle was growing noisy. It swept along the sidelines toward Mr. Devlin, his teammates screaming to psych each other up.

"They said don't call the police!" Mrs. Devlin said.

Mr. Devlin pressed the headphone further into his ear. "Say again? It's tough to hear!"

"No police! They're serious, Hal. A dog dropped off some of Chuckie's clothing."

"They've got a dog working for them?"

"Apparently. Chickie's trying to track him down. But, Hal — "

The team's fullback playfully butted Mr. Devlin in the stomach. The coach stared at him angrily. "Look, I have to go," Mr. Devlin said. "Do what you think is best. It's . . . it's probably just a hoax."

"Hal! Chuckie's our son!"

Now his teammates were swarming around him, butting helmets like billy goats, slapping shoulder pads. Mr. Devlin was being pushed from side to side. "I — I gotta go!" he shouted.

He took the headphones off and gave them back to the coach, just as the team broke their huddle with a loud animal growl.

"Everything okay, Devlin?" the coach asked.

"Sure, Coach," Mr. Devlin said softly. "Just a pep talk from the wife."

The coach smiled. "That's the ticket."

Mr. Devlin looked down at Chuckie's hand-tooled belt, which he had carefully threaded through the loops of his pants. The word *DAD* stared back at him.

"Tell me, Coach," he said, gently touching the belt, "what's more important to you, football or family?"

"Are you kidding?" the coach said with a laugh. "Football's my life!"

Mr. Devlin nodded slowly. "That's what I thought."

He grabbed a football, teed it up, and uncorked a powerful kick. The ball soared through the air — and clear over the entire practice net.

The coach looked at him, shocked. But Mr. Devlin's face was set with determination. He knew exactly what he was going to do.

Chapter 17

The sports announcer's voice crackled over a portable radio in the warehouse office:

"*. . . and with less than a minute to go on the third quarter, Devlin will try a thirty-two-yard field goal that could put the Packers ahead. . . . There's the snap . . . the kick's up . . .*"

Lennie and Eli huddled closer, their ears pressed to the radio.

"*. . . and it's wide! No good! Devlin's second miss from inside the thirty-five. And this game is still scoreless!*"

"Wooooo-haaaaaah!"

With a howl of triumph, Lennie and Eli slapped high fives.

Plop!

A hollow noise from inside the warehouse made them stop. Eli grabbed a flashlight. Slowly he walked through the door into the warehouse, with Lennie close behind.

As Eli moved his arm left and right, the flashlight

beam swept across the room. Wispy clouds of dust seemed to hang in the stagnant air.

Then the light landed on Chuckie. He was sitting in the same place, bound with the same rope, gagged with the same handkerchief.

But his Packer cap and Packer shirt were missing — and so were both of his tennis shoes.

One of the shoes was on the floor, at the very edge of the light's circle. Eli focused the light on it.

He stepped toward it, his face and body tense. "What the — " he began.

Plop!

Eli leaped backward, startled, as the other shoe dropped from above.

He swung the flashlight upward. The light passed across a network of wooden rafters, making long, eerie shadows.

And then the light stopped. There, on one of the rafters, was a small, crouched figure.

Bingo.

Before Eli could react, Bingo attacked. Springing off his hind feet, he leapt onto Eli's shoulder. With a cry of surprise, Eli tumbled to the ground. The flashlight clattered away, its light jerking from wall to wall.

"Lennie!" Eli shrieked. "Get him off me!"

Lennie jumped in to help. The three of them rumbled on the floor in a mass of flying fists, feet, and fur.

Chuckie stared at them, panicked. He knew he'd have to get free. Bingo wasn't an attack dog. He could *distract* Lennie and Eli, but in the long run he couldn't possibly be a match for them.

Chuckie lurched left and right in his chair, throwing all his weight into the effort. The ropes cut into his skin. He tried to shake them off, loosen his hands, *anything*. . . .

But for all their flaws, Lennie and Eli knew how to tie a rope. The harder he tried, the tighter it seemed to get.

Sweat seemed to pour out of him. He wasn't getting anywhere. His sudden glimmer of hope was fast turning into a black feeling of doom.

He had no idea that they were all being watched. . . .

Through a warehouse window, beyond the jagged shadows of machinery, Chickie stared in frozen disbelief. His eyes were as wide as cue balls.

He jumped back to the ground and ran. His feet had never moved so fast. In minutes he was home, barging through the front door. "Mom!" he yelled. "I found him!"

Mrs. Devlin's eyes were fixed on the TV. Her hands reached absentmindedly into a half-empty bowl of popcorn. "Found who?" she asked without looking up.

"Chuckie! They've got him in a warehouse with a bomb and — "

"Ssshhhhh!"

On the TV, the Packers were lined up for a field goal. The TV announcer's voice was tense with anticipation.

". . . *Devlin attempts a twenty-two-yard field goal, his third attempt of the day. . . . The snap is*

*good . . . no one's near him . . . and the kick is . . .
wide left! Still no score going into the fourth
quarter — and let me tell you, it's a good thing for
Devlin his teammates aren't armed. . . ."*

Chickie jumped in front of the TV. "Mother!" he
shouted as loud as he could. "I found Chuckie!"

Mrs. Devlin snapped out of her trance. "Oh, my
God! Where?"

"Some old warehouse. We've got to call the police — now!"

"I can't do that!" Mrs. Devlin said, remembering
what the kidnappers had told her.

"We've got no choice!" Chickie insisted. "They'll
kill him!"

Mrs. Devlin looked at him, her panic mixed with
a sudden tenderness. "You're . . . genuinely *concerned* about your brother, aren't you?"

Chickie glanced away. "Well . . . with him gone,
I figure I'd have to take twice as much grief from
you and Dad."

At the warehouse, the fighting had stopped. Bingo's rescue attempt had failed. Chuckie was still
bound and gagged. Bingo paced the floor, whining,
on a leash tied to Chuckie's chair.

Lennie crouched near the chair. As he fiddled
with the timer in his suitcase, he softly sang, "There
was a farmer had a dog, and — "

"Shut up with that song!" Eli said, taking a cigar
out of his mouth.

"I can't get it out of my head," Lennie said with
a shrug.

Eli pitched his cigar over his shoulder. It disappeared behind a pile of cardboard boxes. "Is this ready?" he asked impatiently. "I want to push the button."

"Hey, *I'm* the technician here," Lennie protested. "*I* push the button."

He stood back from the open suitcase, holding the remote controller. As he proudly watched Eli inspect the bomb, he said, "Carry-on size, but enough wallop to level a city block. And we can trigger the timer from miles away."

With a vengeful smirk, Eli leaned toward Bingo and sang, "There was a crook that had a bomb and — *ka-blooey*!"

Giggling, Lennie picked up the suitcase, closed it, and threw it into a tall bin — a bin that contained dozens of identical-looking suitcases.

As the two crooks stood up and ran out of the warehouse, their laughter rang through the rafters.

Chuckie was pale. His mouth felt dry and parched. But it wasn't the bomb that was bothering him right then.

It was the smoke.

From among the boxes, right where Eli had thrown his cigar, a small plume of smoke was rising. Below it he could see a tongue of yellow flame, which was growing bigger by the second.

Chapter 18

"There they are!" Chickie said to Sheriff Conally as Lennie and Eli ran out of the warehouse.

The sheriff nodded. He, Chickie, and Mrs. Devlin peered intently through his windshield. They watched the two crooks jump into their Chevy and peel out of the parking lot.

Wasting no time, Sheriff Conally steered his squad car out from behind a nearby building. He sped into town, tailing the Chevy. The two cars screeched around corners and streaked down streets, their motors roaring. The Packer game, which had been blaring out of the sheriff's radio, was being drowned out by the engine. He leaned forward to turn it up.

"Can't you go any faster?" Chickie yelled over the noise.

"You want me to blow my engine?" the sheriff asked.

"You want my old man to miss another field goal?" Chickie shouted.

The sheriff floored the accelerator, and the car sped up with a jolt.

In the Chevy, Lennie and Eli listened intently to the game.

"*. . . and the referee starts the clock with four minutes left. . . .*"

In response, Lennie pressed the remote controller.

All along the street, garage doors received the signal and opened wide.

And in the warehouse, the timer began its countdown along with the game's: 4:00 . . . 3:59 . . . 3:58 . . .

Chuckie swallowed hard. Beside him, Bingo was furiously gnawing at his leash.

With a few vicious bites, Bingo chewed all the way through and broke loose. Then he ran to Chuckie and began to work on his rope.

"Bingo, it's no use!" Chuckie yelled, his voice still muffled by the gag.

Bingo looked at him curiously. He jumped onto Chuckie's lap and pulled the gag out of his mouth.

"I said it's no use!" Chuckie blurted. "Try to break the fire alarm. Over there, boy!"

He jerked his head toward the smoldering boxes.

Bingo followed Chuckie's gaze. Mounted on a far wall was a red alarm with a glass bar.

There was only one problem. To get to it, Bingo would have to climb on some of the factory equipment, then leap over a stack of boxes — boxes that were beginning to smoke. And where there was smoke, Bingo knew there would soon be fire.

Fire.

Bingo's old fear was coming back. The fear that had gotten him kicked out of the circus.

"Well, go on!" Chuckie shouted. "You can get up there and break the glass. You can do it, Bingo! You've got to!"

Bingo went to the equipment and looked up. Slowly he climbed onto an old conveyor. He hopped onto a rusty control panel and then a long, horizontal girder.

The girder was narrow, but it stretched right past the smoking boxes that were near the fire alarm. If Bingo was lucky, and quick, with a strong jump he could clear the boxes and swipe the fire alarm with his paw. He crouched down, ready to jump.

And then the boxes burst into flame.

Bingo started to shake. He looked helplessly back at Chuckie.

"That's it, Bingo," Chuckie said, starting to feel woozy from the smoke. "Jump the boxes, break the glass! What's wrong, boy?"

Images flashed into Bingo's mind. He saw Steve, screaming at him to jump through the Ring of Fire. He saw the flames in his puppyhood pet shop, leaping all around him. He saw himself, howling at his mother's grave.

He couldn't do it.

He looked back again at Chuckie. Chuckie's eyes

bore into him deeply. They understood, somehow. They knew the pain Bingo was going through. They also understood the consequences.

Yes, we are both about to die.

That's what Chuckie's eyes were saying when they fluttered closed.

Chapter 19

Chuckie slumped in his chair, overcome by smoke inhalation. His panicked face was now lifeless, at peace.

Bingo recognized that look — it was on Chuckie's face the day Bingo had rescued him from the stream. Chuckie's heart had stopped beating that day. Bingo had brought him back to life — and, now, because of Bingo, Chuckie was about to die.

Again.

Bingo paced the girder, whimpering with terror. Flames danced underneath him, rose up around him like a funeral pyre.

He saw Chuckie's chest rising and falling . . . rising and falling. . . . Chuckie was still alive. But how long would that last? A minute? An hour?

A thought burst its way into Bingo's mind, crowding out all the others: *There's more hope now than there was that day at the stream. He was dead then — but he's alive now.*

Bingo turned away from Chuckie. He stared at

the fire alarm, which seemed to jiggle like Jell-O in the hot, rising currents of the fire.

He's alive now. . . .

Bingo walked to the end of the girder, away from the fire. He crouched low, feeling about twenty degrees cooler.

Then, with an explosive burst of speed, he started running.

Toward the boxes.

His temperature rose. His field of vision turned orange-yellow. The alarm was now a tiny jot of metal beyond the blaze. Bingo planted his feet and sprang off the girder.

He soared in the air. The flames licked the fur on his belly, making it shrivel and blacken. The wall was all but invisible.

Then his paws hit something. Something lumpy and hard. In that split second Bingo's sense of touch told him he had landed on the fire alarm. He swiped his paw downward.

With a barely audible tinkle, the glass bar shattered and fell to the floor.

And so did Bingo.

Across town, Lennie was leading the sheriff through the streets at eighty miles an hour. "Can't you get him off our tail?" Eli shouted.

"Watch this!" Lennie shouted. He yanked the steering wheel to the right. The Chevy's right side lifted off the ground. Eli lurched to the left, jamming into Lennie's shoulder.

They cleared the corner onto a side street — and

came grill-to-grill with a police blockade.

Skrrreeeeeeeeeeee. . . .

Lennie jammed on the brakes. The car fishtailed to one side, then the other. Cops leapt out of their cars and dived for the sidewalks.

As the Chevy screeched to a stop, inches from the blockade, only one sound could be heard — the Packer game, blaring from every car radio.

"*. . . and the Packers stop the clock again with forty seconds remaining. . . .*"

Lennie quickly picked up his remote controller and clicked it. A loud, rumbling metallic noise resounded along the street. All the neighborhood garages around them, which had been gaping open, were closing in unison.

"*. . . and Devlin is coming onto the field to attempt a fifty-four-yarder. . . .*"

"What are you doing?" Eli said. "We're trapped, and you're playing with that stupid remote!"

"You're not my boss!" Lennie shot back. He held the remote up, clicking it again and again. "Now the kid's hamburger, now he's not," he chanted in a singsong voice. "Now he is, now he's not. . . ."

Shielded behind the door of his squad car, the sheriff yelled through a bullhorn, "Let the boy go, and nobody'll be hurt!"

Eli stuck his head out his window. "Make sure Devlin misses the field goal," he shouted, "and the kid'll stay safe and sound."

The sheriff lifted his bullhorn again. "Let me think about it," he replied.

"Think about it?" Mrs. Devlin screamed. "What's

to think about? What about my boy?"

Without answering her, the sheriff leaned into his car and grabbed his radio mike. "Dispatcher," he said into it, "patch me through to the Silverdome. It's a major emergency."

"What are you doing?" Mrs. Devlin demanded.

"First things first," the sheriff said.

Mrs. Devlin's mouth dropped again. In the shocked silence, the radio announcer's voice continued.

"... and now Green Bay has called another timeout. They want Devlin to think about this kick. And in the meantime, it looks like Devlin's being called to the sidelines. . . ."

"Yeah?" Mr. Devlin's voice crackled over the police radio.

"This is Sheriff Conally calling from Green Bay," the sheriff said into the mike. "We've got your son, and everything is going to be okay, so go out there and nail this field goal for Chuckie."

"You bet!" Mr. Devlin replied, his voice suddenly filled with relief. "Thanks, Sheriff!"

Before the sheriff could hang up, Mrs. Devlin began beating him on the back. "How could you say that?" she shrieked. "You liar, you murderer — "

"Come on, lady," the sheriff said, pushing her away. "A lot of us have money on this game. Besides, I think these clowns are bluffing."

"Time's running out, Sheriff!" came Eli's voice from the Chevy.

The sheriff grabbed his bullhorn. "Okay, okay!" he shouted. "But, first, I want to see the kid."

"He's not here!" Eli yelled back.

"Not here?" the sheriff bellowed. "Where is he?"

"You'll find him, in due time," Eli said with a cackle of glee. "What condition you find him in depends on the game. . . ."

Chapter 20

When Chuckie awoke, he was lying on the floor of the warehouse. Two faces loomed over him — two men in fire fighters' gear.

Beside the bin that contained the suitcase-bomb, Bingo was barking hysterically.

"What's with that dog?" one fire fighter asked Chuckie.

"Forget the dog," the other one said. "Call the paramedics!"

Chuckie blinked. He looked around, dazed. Slowly it all came back to him. The fire . . . it was out — Bingo had somehow tripped the alarm. Chuckie's bonds . . . they were untied. The bomb . . .

Chuckie sat bolt upright. He looked at Bingo. "Wait! A bomb! There's a bomb in the suitcase in that bin! They can blow it up from anywhere!"

One of the fire fighters went to the bin and tipped it over. With a dull clatter, suitcases tumbled out by the dozen.

"This was a suitcase factory, kid," the fire fighter said. "Which one is it?"

"Bingo!" Chuckie yelled. "You have to find it!"

Bingo darted to the suitcases, sniffing them frantically. Finally he put his paw on one of them.

"You sure?" Chuckie asked. "I think it's the one next to it!"

"Rowf!" Bingo barked.

"Okay, okay!" Chuckie said. "Just get rid of it."

Bingo clamped his jaws on the suitcase handle and ran with it out the door. As Chuckie watched him sprint across an open field, his heart felt like it was going to explode from his chest.

Across town, the entire police blockade stood frozen as the play-by-play blasted out into the afternoon air. Mrs. Devlin clutched onto Chickie, barely able to stand on her own.

"... so to break this deadlock, Devlin's going to have to beat his personal best of fifty-three yards. But with forty seconds to go, the Packers have no choice. It's their last chance. Devlin's ready . . . looking confident . . . the snap . . . the kick is up. . . ."

Lennie fiddled with the remote controller. It was off now, but if Devlin made the field goal . . .

"And he missed it! The game is still tied!"

The sheriff dropped his bullhorn in shock. Mrs. Devlin collapsed with relief into her son's arms. The other cops stared at each other, dumbfounded. The neighborhood garage doors stayed shut.

Lennie grinned at Eli. "Hey, it worked! What do you know!"

But the sheriff's face was turning red with anger. His team was supposed to win. Several of his weeks' salaries had just gone up in smoke.

He pulled a rifle out of his car and brought it to his shoulder. Cocking it, he took aim at Eli. "You dirty, stinking — "

"Sheriff, no!" Mrs. Devlin screamed.

The rifle went off. A bullet blazed toward the Chevy.

"Yeeeeow!" Lennie yelled. He grabbed his right hand in excruciating pain.

The remote controller flew out of his hand. It sailed through the car window and crashed to the street.

Up and down the street, the neighborhood garages began to trundle open.

"It . . . it turned on . . ." Chickie said.

KAAAAAAA-BOOOOOOOOOM! The explosion was distant, but very, very loud.

But there was one sound even louder.

Mrs. Devlin's horrified scream.

Chapter 21

Chuckie was awake — sort of. His eyes were closed, but he was thinking. Things were coming back to him, little by little. He was in a hospital bed, that much he knew. The fire fighters had taken him there. After the explosion. After the blast that flashed outside the warehouse.

When he saw that blast, a part of him went dead. What had happened then? An ambulance, this hospital, some doctors asking him questions — important questions . . . but about what?

He felt his eyelids flickering. He began to hear voices.

"Is he all right?" someone was saying.

"Can we talk to him?" someone else said.

He opened his eyes. Looming over him was his dad — his broad shoulders crowding his mom, Chickie, and Dr. Frick to the side.

"Hey, partner," Hal Devlin said with a warm smile. "It's your old man."

"Dad?" was all Chuckie could manage, his voice tiny and hoarse.

"You'd have been proud of your father, Chuckie," his mom said. "He kicked a fifty-two yarder in overtime to win the game."

"Well, that was nothing," Mr. Devlin said. "Nothing compared to what Chuckie did. That was quite a gesture, son, donating a kidney to a dog. Kind of dumb, but . . . very generous."

"That's not just any dog, Dad," Chickie said. "Bingo's a real hero!"

That was it! Chuckie remembered it all now. Bingo had survived, barely. He had needed an immediate kidney transplant in order to live, and Chuckie had agreed to do it.

"How . . . how is Bingo?" Chuckie asked.

"It's touch and go," Dr. Frick said. "The blast blew a lot of fuzz off him, but thank God the bomb wasn't in that cheap soft-sided luggage, or there wouldn't have been anything to transplant your kidney into."

"Can I see him?" Chuckie asked.

"Sure." Dr. Frick disappeared a moment, then came back with a wheelchair. Chuckie's dad lifted him in and wheeled him down the hall. Dr. Frick went ahead and held open the door of another hospital room.

As Chuckie rolled in, a huge crowd of people turned around. Chuckie knew some of them, but the rest were total strangers.

Lennie and Eli stood side by side, wearing handcuffs, with Sheriff Conally close by. Mrs. Grimbleby turned and gave him a prickly faced smile.

Steve and Ginger were there, with the three Hollywood Poodles — and so were Duke and Emma Lois, wearing aprons that said DUKE'S VEGETARIAN DINER. The Thompson family was off to the side, along with Foureyes, Bunny, Vic, the judge who had sentenced Bingo, the defense attorney, the prosecutor, and the traffic cop who had stopped Bingo way back in Denver.

"Who are all these people?" Chuckie asked.

His mom smiled. "They all heard Bingo's story on the nightly news and wanted to wish him well."

Chuckie grabbed the wheels of his chair and rolled further into the room. The crowd backed away to give him space, everyone smiling respectfully.

Lennie held up his cuffed hand to show that his fingers were crossed for good luck.

Eli grinned and said, "Hope your dog doesn't die!"

Duke offered Chuckie a carrot stick and dip.

But Chuckie ignored them all. His eyes were focused on the white curtain drawn across the bed in the middle of the room.

As Chuckie got nearer, he saw there was someone inside with Bingo. A wrinkled hand grabbed the curtain from within and pulled it aside.

Chuckie's heart took a jump. There was Bingo. He was lying motionlessly in bed, covered with bandages and hooked up to several monitors. His eyes were closed, and he was breathing with difficulty.

But he was alive.

The man standing over him was tall, gray-haired,

and kindly, a dead-ringer for Captain Kangaroo. "He's yours, now," the man said. "Take good care of him."

"Who are you?" Chuckie asked.

"Bingo's old master," the man answered. "You know . . . there was a farmer had a dog and Bingo was his name-o . . ."

Chuckie's eyes widened. *"That* farmer?"

"Yep."

"How did you two get separated?"

The man chuckled. "That's a whole other story, son."

Chuckie smiled and wheeled himself right up to Bingo's bed. He put his hand on Bingo's bandaged paw, then stroked his head. "Oh, Bingo, you just have to pull through," he said, his voice breaking. "I need you, boy."

Suddenly Bingo's eyes popped open. He blinked once, then turned his head. He stared at Chuckie, then let out a sudden "Rowf!"

Chuckie felt like jumping with happiness. A murmur swept through the crowd. Dr. Frick examined Bingo and said, "I think he's going to be just fine, Chuckie, thanks to you."

Chuckie bent forward over the bed. "Oh, Bingo," he cried out, gently putting his arms around him. "Can I keep him, Dad? Can I?"

The room fell silent. All eyes turned to Mr. Devlin.

He furrowed his brow and cleared his throat. The toes on his famous bare foot twitched uncomfortably. Chuckie swallowed, expecting the worst.

"Sure, son," Mr. Devlin finally said with a smile. "Heck, after today, I'm going to buy him season tickets!"

Cheers rang out in the hospital room. People clapped Mr. Devlin on the back.

And Chuckie just held on to Bingo, laughing and crying and feeling like his life was finally, finally on the right track.